BOOKER & FITCH

MURDER
at
Work

LIZ HEDGECOCK PAULA HARMON

WHITE
RHINO
BOOKS

Copyright © Liz Hedgecock, Paula Harmon, 2024

All rights reserved. Apart from any use permitted under UK copyright law, no part of this publication may be reproduced, stored in a retrieval system, or transmitted, in any form or by any means, electronic, mechanical, photocopying, recording or otherwise, without the prior written permission of the copyright owner.

This is a work of fiction. Names, characters, businesses, places, events and incidents are either the products of the author's imagination or used in a fictitious manner. Any resemblance to actual persons, living or dead, or actual events is purely coincidental.

ISBN-13: 979-8326535542

*To all our lovely readers!
Thank you for your support and
encouragement*

CHAPTER 1

'That,' said Jade, 'was a very profitable morning.' She pressed a button on the old-fashioned cash register which she had recently purchased. It was meant to be a treat for the shop, but she knew it was a piece of self-indulgence. With a pleasing *ping*, the cash drawer shot out. She touched the piles of banknotes sitting in their little trays.

'It was,' said Netta. 'We've had seven online orders and another ten people signed up for our subscription box over the weekend. That's a hundred and seventy.'

'Lovely.' Jade rubbed her hands and closed the till drawer. 'Will you want to get the orders out today?'

'If we've got everything in, definitely. I'll check while it's quiet.' Netta hunkered behind the screen of her laptop.

Now that Netta had implemented a stock-control

database, Jade rather missed the ritual of wandering into the back room and rummaging through stacks of cardboard boxes to conduct a stocktake. As it was, Netta generally pounced on her whenever she came back from the storage shed with stock for the shelves, demanding to know what Jade had taken so that she could update the records. Occasionally Jade felt as if she was playing gooseberry in the complex relationship between Netta and the shop's stock.

After a couple of minutes, Netta peeped round the screen. 'We can fulfil today's orders, but we'll definitely have to put in a big order for this month's subscription boxes. And we need small white envelopes to fit our gift vouchers. For some reason, three were requested online.'

'Maybe they're buying for someone who's planning a trip to Hazeby-on-Wyvern,' said Jade. 'I don't pretend to understand our customers, but as long as they're buying from us, I don't mind.' She looked at the clock. 'I could nip out and buy envelopes now, if you want. I'm distinctly peckish.' She picked up a gift voucher from the rack by the till. 'I'm taking one for measurement,' she said hastily, in case Netta started updating one of her spreadsheets.

'Oh, would you?' said Netta. 'Then I can do the online orders later while you serve and get them to the post office for last collection.' A dreamy look came over her face. 'Maybe one day we can set up end-to-end automation…'

'Right, I'm heading out,' said Jade, before Netta went off on one of her techno-utopian business dreams. *It's probably my own fault for introducing her to Hugo,* she thought, as she got her swirly black coat from the stand and added a long purple woolly scarf, matching gloves and bobble hat.

It was a crisp autumn day, the kind that calls for steaming hot chocolate with marshmallows. *Maybe I'll treat myself. I could get one for Netta, too. But first, the envelopes.*

She strode along, swishing through occasional piles of rustling leaves, until she reached the post office. There were probably cheaper envelopes to be had in Hazeby, if she chose to seek them, but given the number of times Jim visited Crystal Dreams to deliver parcels or pick them up, Jade felt the postal services in general deserved her support.

'Afternoon!' she called, and went to peer at the shelves, gift voucher in hand. A pack of suitable envelopes selected, she took them to the counter.

'Afternoon, Jade,' said Moira, taking the envelopes in a red-nailed hand dripping with gold jewellery and scanning them. 'Anything else you need? Packing tape, boxes?'

Jade smiled. 'All taken care of, Moira. Crystal Dreams is a finely tuned machine, thanks to Netta.'

'You're very cheerful,' observed Moira. She

regarded Jade, her mouth pulled down slightly. Her long upper lip gave her the look of an elegant horse.

'I'm usually cheerful,' said Jade. 'Besides, it's a lovely day and I think Crystal Dreams will have the best Halloween ever.'

Moira's eyebrows drew together slightly. 'This is only the shop's second year, isn't it?'

'Well, if you're being picky,' said Jade, grinning. 'OK then, my best *business* Halloween ever.'

'Let's hope so,' said Moira. 'That's three ninety-nine, please.'

Jade took her envelopes and the receipt and headed out. That was a point – she hadn't even thought about the shop's Halloween window display yet. It was early October: high time she got something together. Particularly as Halloween was a magic shop's Christmas. She strolled, window gazing. Maybe some velvet… Purple or orange, or maybe teal? Was teal a step too far? How much would they need? She went into Sew Crafty, the haberdasher's, and stroked the bolts of fabric. Velvet was expensive, but they could always reuse it. Or perhaps repurpose it? Netta would probably have ideas… She took photos of different-coloured velvets and made a note of the prices per metre on her phone. Later she'd transfer the information to her master notebook, black with silver stars, which lived in the drawer of the shop counter.

'Anything I can help you with?' called Sandra,

from the far end of the long, narrow shop. She seemed small and lost, as if Jade was looking through the wrong end of a telescope.

'I'm pricing velvet for a Halloween window display,' said Jade. 'I'm not sure how much I need. I'll have to measure up.'

'I suppose you will,' said Sandra. 'Anything's worth a try, isn't it?'

Jade frowned. 'We use fabric in the window quite often.'

'You do,' said Sandra. 'Oh, it's a cut-throat world and no mistake.' She looked as sententious as someone in a pink pinny possibly could.

Jade drew herself up. 'Things are going well at the moment, but we're not competing with you. If that's what you mean.'

'No, dear,' said Sandra. 'You give me a ring when you know what you want. I'll see you right. Unlike some.' She gave Jade an owlish nod.

'Will do,' said Jade, and left feeling bewildered.

'What's got into her?' she muttered, as she headed down the street. Then she caught sight of the sandwich board on the pavement outside Betsy's, which put Sandra out of her head completely. *A bacon sandwich will cheer me up. Possibly with mushrooms, which makes it healthy. And a hot chocolate – no, two.* She joined the short queue and shuffled along, her mouth watering at the smell of good things which wafted from inside the café.

Betsy herself was serving. 'Hello there, Jade. How are things with you?'

'All good, thanks,' said Jade, beaming at her. 'Tickety boo.'

'Marvellous. What can I get you?'

Jade placed her order and paid. 'That's gone through,' said Betsy. 'I'm glad to see you so chirpy, considering.'

'Considering what?' *Have I missed something?*

Betsy put her head on one side. 'You haven't heard?'

'Heard what?'

Betsy looked cagey, as if considering whether or not to spill the beans, then relented. 'Believe it or not, someone's finally taken on old Mr Darcy's place. When he retired, I thought that shop would crumble into dust.'

'Someone's taken on Ye Olde Wyvern Booke Shoppe?' Jade wasn't sure whether to be pleased or not.

Her friend Fi, who owned the Book Barge by the river, had been conscience-stricken when the news came out that Mr Darcy was shutting up shop. 'I hope I didn't drive him out of business,' she said. 'If it was a chain, that would be different. I hate to think that I might have helped shut down an independent bookshop.'

'You read too much into these things,' said Jade. 'The Book Barge is an independent bookshop, for heaven's sake. Anyway, Mr Darcy didn't like it when people bought things. He preferred having the books to himself. Now he's retired, he can.'

'I suppose,' Fi had replied, seeming unconvinced.

Jade realised Betsy hadn't answered her question. 'Is Mr Darcy's bookshop under new management?'

'The bookshop? Not as such,' said Betsy, looking everywhere but at Jade. 'Maybe you should check it out.'

'Maybe I will.' Jade moved to the end of the counter, her brain working furiously. Luckily, her order was ready quickly. She grabbed the paper bag with her sandwich, balanced the cardboard drinks holder, and hurried off.

Suddenly, the street was full of obstacles – people getting in her way, bollards and lamp posts coming out of nowhere, not to mention planters and litter bins whose corners seemed specially designed to catch a hip or a knee. Jade battled on, driven by a growing sense of foreboding, ignoring even the growling of her stomach in her quest.

She turned down Market Street and strode on, looking for the familiar bow-fronted window with its peeling, yellowing frame.

It wasn't there.

No, the *window* was there, its frame now glistening

with fresh purple paint. The interior of the shop was hidden by black fabric draped inside the window – Sandra's bolts of fabric flashed into Jade's mind – and a poster was stuck in the middle of the glass. It proclaimed, in curly bright-pink lettering: *OPENING SATURDAY – YOUR NEW BRANCH OF MAGICAL MOMENTS!*

Jade gasped. This more than explained the odd encounters she had had today. Of all the shops to open in Hazeby, another magic shop. Worse, it was part of a chain. An *international* chain. She closed her eyes, counted to three, then opened them, hoping it had been a trick of her imagination.

No: the sign was still there.

Deep discounts, thought Jade. *Two-for-one offers. Economies of scale. Good grief, I sound like Netta.*

She took a deep breath, but it was no good. The cups of hot chocolate were juddering in their holder. She looked down and saw her hand trembling. *I just— Oh no. Not now. Not when everything is going so well.* And she hurried away before anyone else could make a wise observation or sympathise with her.

CHAPTER 2

Fi paused as she bagged up the cozy romance that Mrs Brummell was buying from the Book Barge. The title suggested a gentle story about a mini-break, full of silly misunderstandings, gentle kisses and happy endings. On its cover, an attractive couple drove towards an unspecified coastline in an unspecified convertible, the woman's long hair flowing behind her in complete disregard of physics and also of how painful it would be to brush the tangles out later.

It was a hundred times less racy than Mrs Brummell's normal fare.

Fi rarely read romance of any kind, but her thoughts returned to the weekend: walking along the beach hand in hand with Marcus, sea spray on their faces as they kissed while Stan the dog chased seagulls, then watching the autumn sunset from their hotel room. She sighed before she could stop herself.

'I hope you don't think that book's for me,' said Mrs Brummell, her lips narrowing as she extracted her purse from a sensible handbag. 'It's for my great-niece, who's rather prim. I don't know what young people are coming to. I wouldn't read anything so tame if you paid me.'

'Each to their own,' said Fi, with a grin. 'I'm just back from a mini-break myself. It already feels like a million years ago.'

'I hope you had more fun than the characters in this book, and that you had more sense than to travel in an open-top car with the roof down. Apparently the British have more convertibles per population than anywhere in the world, despite the weather, which proves that we're—'

'Optimists,' said Fi, firmly. 'It was a lovely couple of days and we went in a perfectly average car. Roof, heating, comfort. Nice and r—' She realised she was about to say romantic and felt herself blush. She was all too aware of Mrs Brummell's smirk, the customers nearby, and Nerys openly listening from the galley, where she was making coffee. It would be bad enough putting up with Jade's mocking sniggers later. She and Marcus had only been serious for a few months. 'Nice and relaxing. That'll be eight ninety-nine, please.'

'Is your lad helping with Blithe Spirit at the Little Theatre?' Mrs Brummell put her change in the St Jude's Homeless Shelter charity tin by the till and the book in her bag. 'Let's hope the only drama on stage this year is the actual play. Cheerio! Don't forget to email me when *my* book is in.'

'I will,' said Fi, suppressing another sigh. In the course of their brief discussion, the short break with Marcus had faded even further. Dylan was indeed helping backstage at the theatre again, and from what he'd said, rehearsals with the small but talented amateur-dramatic troupe were going well. What was left of the previous company, after a murder the previous year during their production of *Macbeth*, had departed on a national tour, and the former leading lady was rumoured to be rehearsing for a TV drama.

Fi had asked Dylan if the new troupe might be headed for stardom, but he'd merely shrugged. Trying to gather useful information about any of the million things he was doing these days – playing his own gigs, helping at Rick's, going to parties, and occasionally doing sixth-form schoolwork – was like trying to piece together a whole garment from a few patches of frayed fabric.

Nerys placed the shop's laptop on the counter. 'Can't wait till Chester's sixteen and me and Liam will be free in the evenings. The school sends a million emails a day.'

'Mmm,' said Fi. It was pointless to burst Nerys's bubble about motherhood turning into an easy ride later. She remembered feeling the same way when

Dylan was six. Maybe there were only half a million emails a day now and yes, she was free in the evenings. But the worrying hadn't stopped… Then there was Marcus, whose son Leo was planning to work for an independent trekking company when he'd finished his A levels. At weekends, Leo spent more time out of mobile range than Dylan did with a flat battery.

'Thanks so much for taking charge when I was away, Nerys,' said Fi, to change the subject. 'Sales were really good. Please tell me when you want time off. Especially as your mum's offered to have the children for a weekend.'

'I can't leave you to manage alone. You haven't had a break today.'

'I won't be alone,' said Fi. 'Zach isn't at college *all* the time. In fact, he'll be back in a minute, then I'll take a break. You should look after yourself and Liam. It's important.'

'I'd feel bad leaving the kids.'

'The kids will have a lovely time. Everyone needs a change sometimes.'

'I guess.' Nerys's finger made circles on the lid of the laptop. 'Zach wants to change the oojamaflip.'

Fi raised her eyebrows and waited for clarification. Zach wouldn't do anything like that without asking her, any more than Nerys would. And Fi would have the final word: Nerys knew that. So why was she letting the oojamaflip, whatever that was, bother her? And why hadn't she mentioned it earlier?

A tap on the counter made her jump. A man in his late twenties with a battered backpack grinned at her. 'Books on the philosophy of gaming?' he said.

'Oh, er, yes,' said Fi. 'The gaming section is new.' She pointed to the area which had contained books about magic, a subject she'd given up so that she could send people to Crystal Dreams. 'My assistant will join you in a moment.'

Nerys snorted as Zach descended the steps. 'Perhaps Game Boy can help.'

'No, you can,' said Fi. 'You and Liam game as much as Zach and Dylan. Be proud of your knowledge.'

'We don't get all brainiac about it.'

'Good, then you won't get bogged down and you're more likely to sell something.'

'You could have bought old Mr Darcy's shop and opened a board-game café. Zach could put his skills to use there.' Nerys put on a bright smile and went to help the customer, brushing past Zach on the way.

'How was college, Zach?' Fi asked.

'Fine, thanks. Did you have a good break?'

'Lovely. Um…'

Zach stowed his things and moved behind the till as Fi collected her coat and Stan. 'Jade's heading this way. I'd have walked over with her, but that might have made me late back. Hey, is that a customer in the gaming section?'

Fi followed his gaze and saw Nerys watching them, her face neutral. 'Zach, was everything all right when I was on holiday?'

'Yup. Me and Nerys have got ideas to run past you. Nerys is working out what I've forgotten to include.'

'Is she?'

'She went a bit thoughtful when I said what I'd been thinking, so yeah.' Zach's face was bright and innocent. 'Go on, take your break. I'm ready to take over.'

'Thanks. Um, can you make sure Nerys knows this is a joint plan, not a solo venture?'

'Yeah, course.'

Fi shrugged herself into her coat and left, Stan trotting at her heels. Jade would text if she intended to visit. It would be nice to take Stan for a walk in the cold, clean air and shake off her nostalgia for the weekend. Romantic, indeed. When had she become so sentimental?

She looked away from the river rushing through Hazeby and visualised Mr Darcy's old shop. Several people in town had hoped it would modernise and become a board-game café or an escape room. Several had hinted that Fi, who supported new ideas for Hazeby, could do it. Nerys hadn't mentioned it until today.

It was a good idea, but quite apart from the fact that Fi could never afford to lease the shop, let alone run it, bricks and mortar were too tying. She was happy to be moored to the riverbank. After years juggling a corporate job with raising a child alone, now she had some freedom. She might never leave Hazeby – but she could one day if she wanted to.

Then, through the gap in the flood-defence wall, Fi saw Jade hurrying towards her, the purple bobble on her hat bouncing as she rushed forward. Even from several metres away and in late-afternoon light, Fi could see Jade's clenched jaw: the sort of expression that generally indicates anxiety as much as anger.

Fi strode forward and was nearly bowled over as Jade failed to stop in time. 'Woah, what's happened? Is something wrong with Hugo?'

'What? No!' Jade was trembling. 'I mean, I don't know. But it's not that, it's worse. Or not worse, but almost as bad. It's the end of everything. I might as well give up. Why did I ever think I had the right to things working out?' With every phrase she gesticulated wildly until she risked strangling herself with her own scarf.

'Slow down, Jade.' Fi took her friend's shoulders. 'Is it Rick?'

Stan stood on his hind legs and put his forepaws on Jade's leg. 'Rrrerrfff?'

Jade stared at Fi. 'What's Rick got to do with

anything?'

'The psychic stuff is in your shop,' said Fi. 'I'm just having to guess what's wrong. Have Betsy's or the Duck and Druid gone out of business?'

Jade slumped. 'They haven't,' she said. 'But *I* might as well.' Her voice was full of tears.

'What do you mean? Crystal Dreams is going great guns.'

'It won't now Darcy's has been taken over. You should have done it.'

'I couldn't. Who has?'

'A new branch of Magical Moments.'

'The chain?' Fi relaxed her grip and patted Jade's shoulder. 'That's no competition.'

'How can you say that?'

'Different market. I mean, it's the same market in theory, but a different beast. Some people will never go to an independent shop, but plenty of people won't go to a chain store. They want the unique experience they get from people like you. They don't want identical: they want different. Hazeby has always done well for indies. You'll be fine.'

Jade bit her lip. 'You reckon?'

'Am I ever wrong?'

'You prefer coffee to tea. That's not a good start.' Jade blinked a few times, then scrubbed her eyes with a purple glove. 'You really think so?'

'Come on,' said Fi. 'Let's get something to drink

and talk it over. You'll be fine in no time. I can tell you about my break.'

'Oh yeah.' Jade patted Stan on the head and took Fi's arm. 'Sorry I didn't ask. I suppose it was all romantic, but I bet the photos are good.'

'They're brilliant,' said Fi. 'Lots of slushy selfies of me and Marcus. I can't wait to show you.'

Jade's eyes widened briefly, then she relaxed and made a gagging motion. 'You'd better not.' She attempted a smile.

It shouldn't take long to reassure her, thought Fi. Then she thought of the queue Jade was joining, of Zach, Nerys, Marcus, Leo and Dylan. *Why is it always my job to comfort people?*

CHAPTER 3

'It makes perfect sense,' said Netta. 'Our online business is growing even without advertising. Imagine if I developed several different offers and we started doing low-level advertising on social media. We could maybe send subscription boxes to a few influencers, to extend our reach.'

'We could,' said Jade. 'But how much would this cost? Who's going to do the research, run the adverts, pack the boxes, and keep tabs on it all?' A customer looked round, and she realised her voice had risen to a volume where she could be overheard.

'Well, me,' said Netta, more quietly. 'You made me subscriptions manager – subscriptions and online business manager, really – so I'd just be doing my job. Except for packing the boxes.'

'So who's doing that? Me?' It wasn't that Jade minded hard work, and putting goodies in a few boxes was hardly that. It was the principle of the thing. 'It's not the best use of my time. And who's serving in the shop while this is going on?'

'You did say something not so long ago about getting an extra assistant.'

'That was before Magical Moments came to town,' said Jade. 'I'm not prepared to go through the rigmarole of recruiting another member of staff if I'll have to let them go in a few weeks. It's not fair to them, either. And how am I paying for all this? More stock, advertising and another person in the shop?'

'It would pay for itself in the long run,' said Netta. 'In the meantime, you could either use existing profits or take out a loan. I could do your business case. I've got templates and everything.'

'I'm sure you have,' said Jade, 'but taking out a loan is the last thing I want to do. What if the other shop wipes out Crystal Dreams completely and I'm stuck with a mountain of debt? There'll be interest to pay: it's not free money.'

Netta lifted her chin. 'I know that as well as you do. I thought about going to university, but when I saw how much I'd owe at the end of it…' She looked down for a moment. Then she looked up, with a gleam in her eye which could be a glimmer of victory or the beginnings of a tear. 'If you don't like any of my ideas – and you don't seem to – what do you have in mind? You said we had to do something when you came back from Fi's all fired up.'

'Yes, I did,' said Jade. 'It's not that I don't like your ideas, Netta. It's just that it involves a lot of financial risk and, to be honest, things I don't fully understand. Let me make a brew, then I'll outline what I have in mind.'

'Fine,' said Netta. 'Mine's a camomile.'

'Right you are.'

Jade went into the back room, put the kettle on, and slung two teabags in mugs: one which would produce a proper cup of builder's-strength tea, and another which would have to be left in the mug to ooze out a yellowish liquid which, in Jade's opinion, ought to be poured away rather than drunk. *What do I have in mind?* she thought, as the kettle rumbled at her. *Absolutely nothing.*

That wasn't strictly true. Ever since Netta had suggested extra expenditure, and more specifically a business loan, Jade had been beset by visions of herself, squeezed into a pencil-skirted suit and a narrow plastic chair, sitting in a bank manager's office and being told that due to her horrendous credit history there was no chance of getting a loan. Or alternatively, that they could only offer her one at 250% interest, payable monthly without fail. Or the worst-case scenario: the bank calling her landlord and informing him of the terrible state of her finances, which would of course lead to her landlord throwing her out of both shop and home.

Homeless and jobless. Maybe I could move in with Rick. That wasn't such an awful thought. What was worse was the looks of sympathy she would get as she went about her lack of business in Hazeby. 'She used to have her own shop,' people would whisper, as they waited for her to measure their children's feet or unpack groceries in their porch. 'Then another shop came and her business couldn't cope.' *I'm not having it*, she thought, and the kettle pinged in agreement.

I wish that signalled a bright idea. She filled the mugs and squished her teabag. Not Netta's, because she had learned from experience that Netta's fancy teabags scorned anything but delicate handling and would disintegrate in disgust if they were so much as pressed with a spoon.

What can I do? she thought, as she waited for the tea to brew. *Netta's ideas are so – so big. I need to think of something smaller, but different from what we're doing now.*

Different . . . different... What had she done that was different and had worked? If only she had her notebook: that always helped. It had been an unjustifiable expense at the time: a black hardback notebook with shining silver stars inlaid in the cover and nice thick pages that didn't bleed through. However, it was worth its weight in gold.

Is that it? Unusual items, maybe luxury items?

Handmade or bespoke items that the other shop won't stock?

Look at how well those photo prints do. Last Christmas, she had had a bright idea to take photographs at the winter solstice and make them into framed prints. Admittedly, that had set off a whole chain of events which she preferred not to recall, but the prints themselves had raised lots of money for the local homeless shelter. *So I can do it, it doesn't have to cost a fortune, and it would give local artists and creative people a chance. If I sell them on a consignment basis, it's risk-free. Bingo!* She gave her teabag a celebratory squidge and scored a direct hit to the bin. That had to be a good omen.

She sailed into the shop, bearing mugs. 'So what I have in mind is *this*.' She plonked the mugs on the counter to emphasise the word. 'We diversify our current offering with handmade, bespoke or quirky items which aren't available anywhere else in Hazeby. That will bring people to the shop, and hopefully they'll stock up on our basics while they're here.'

'OK…' said Netta, sipping her anaemic drink. 'What percentage of the shop will you give to this new stuff? Given the cost of living at the moment, can people afford it?'

'Ask the art gallery or the little quirky gift shops,' Jade retorted. 'They're still going and their price tags are steep. And the delicatessen is still selling ridiculously overpriced pasta faster than you can say tagliatelle.' Out of the corner of her eye, she noticed that the customer who had glanced over before was openly watching them. She was wrapped in a large puffer coat which overwhelmed her small frame, not to mention a chunky green scarf and matching beanie, but still, she seemed familiar. And while she had been in the shop for a good few minutes, she had nothing in her hands.

Jade turned to the customer. 'Are you looking for something in particular?'

'Just browsing, thanks.'

Netta put down her mug. 'The art gallery and the gift shops might not like you pinching a share of their market.'

'There's no law against it,' said Jade, 'and as long as the items fit with the rest of my stock, I don't see a problem. Besides, Magical Moments don't seem to be troubled by these concerns, do they?' She made a mental note to find out who had leased them the building, knowing full well that there was already a perfectly good magic-themed shop in Hazeby, and give them a piece of her mind—

Ping! For a moment, Jade thought she had switched the kettle back on by mistake. Then she realised the noise was inside her head. The customer, meanwhile, had moved behind some shelving and was obscured from view.

Netta was opening her mouth to reply, no doubt with an excellent argument, but things had moved on. Jade put a finger to her lips and jerked her head in the direction of the customer.

Netta's eyes widened. 'Shoplifter?' she mouthed.

Jade shook her head. 'Worse.'

She crept forward to see what the customer was doing. She had actually pulled out a little notebook and was writing in it. And the angle she was standing at precisely matched that of her photo on the Magical Moments corporate website.

'Linzi Lawson, I presume,' said Jade, striding towards her. 'Manager of the new Magical Moments store.'

To her credit, the woman didn't jump. She merely closed her notebook. 'That's right.' She extended a hand.

'What do you think you're doing?' Jade replied. 'You're not here to buy, so I assume you're here to snoop. I hope you're not stealing our ideas.'

'You can't arrest me for checking out the competition,' said Linzi. 'I presume you're Jade Fitch, owner of this . . . establishment. In fact, I know you are: I've seen photos of you. And no, I haven't come to steal your ideas. Sure, I've made notes, but I actually came to offer a compromise.'

'Did you now?' Jade felt a hand on her arm. Netta had come to join her. *Does she think I'm going to punch her?* Apart from anything else, she wouldn't do that in front of the customers. Who, of course, had all stopped browsing to watch the show.

'I did. Our business is good at various things – discounts, deals, seasonal items – while your stock is, frankly, niche.' Her lip curled slightly. 'So I'm prepared to stick to what we do best and let you have your herbs and dog toys.'

'Oh, really?' Jade counted to ten in her head, but the last few numbers were very quick indeed. 'Thank you for your offer, but I'll conduct my business in my own way.' She paused, taking in the other woman. 'As far as I'm concerned, this means war.'

Netta's gasp was echoed by some of the customers, who had given up any pretence of concealment and were staring open-mouthed.

Linzi laughed. 'A war you won't win. Since you won't cooperate with my kind offer, here's something to think about. You've done your research on me, sure. But maybe I know a few things about you too, *Jade Fitch.*' She gave Jade a sunny smile and walked out.

'What did that mean?' said Netta.

'Nothing,' said Jade. 'Idle threats. Drink your witches' brew before it goes cold or turns into a frog, whichever comes first.' But underneath her casual manner, her heart was thumping. *She knows about me.*

CHAPTER 9

'Without going into detail,' said Marcus. 'I'm tempted to run away on another short break. Want to come?'

'Without going into detail,' said Fi, 'try and stop me.'

Marcus's apartment was on the top floor of a Georgian building which was all ostentation at the front and utility at the back. In the eighteenth century, the first owners had wanted passers-by to see how rich they were. They desired no connection to a river which was industrial in their day, full of barges laden with grubby goods. A view of it was only fit for the upper windows at the rear of the house.

The apartment was made up of what had once been servants' bedrooms, modernised in keeping with the building's grade II listed status. A small balcony added sometime in the 1950s had been allowed to stay, because it included the fire escape, and looked onto the river as it curved under the upper bridge.

It was a clear if chilly evening. Fi and Marcus sat on the balcony in their coats, cuddling up as they sipped red wine, watching mooring lights dip and dance over boats discernible only by their cosy windows and the strings of coloured lanterns decorating the river's edge.

'Is the new case difficult?' said Fi.

'Intricate, rather than difficult. Lots of fiddly little things to piece together. We'll get there, but it's using a lot of resource from my team. Never mind. What about you? I saw Nerys the day we came back and she had a face like thunder. I nearly didn't recognise her. She usually looks happy, shy or both, not murderous. What have you done?'

'Not me. Zach.' Fi sipped her wine. 'Not even Zach really. I *think* it's sorted. Sort of.'

'What *he* done?'

Fi cuddled closer. 'You know he's late to education because of one thing and another? He hated school. Now he's playing catch-up.'

'Yes.'

'He's at risk of burning out. He's absorbing information and trying to implement a million ideas at the same time.'

'What sort of ideas?' said Marcus.

'He wants to reconfigure everything from the website to my accounts, which I can manage perfectly well before handing them to Stuart. But that's not all. While I was away, he decided we could use AI to restructure the layout of the boat. And he wants to create short videos and work with influencers.'

Marcus choked on his wine. 'Those young women in three inches of make-up who sashay about?'

'Nerys jumped to exactly the same conclusion,' said Fi. 'There's more than one kind of influencer. It's possible to like books as well as fashion, I'll have you know.'

'Yes, but the current case involves a wannabe fashion influencer from Mistleby who we arrested for shoplifting a few months ago. She tried to attack Constable Grace and almost took his eye out with one of her ten-inch nails. Luckily, it got caught in his stab vest and snapped. She's trying to sue us for damage to the tools of her trade.'

'Really?'

'If she gets released, don't pick her. Anyway, why was Nerys so bothered?'

Fi shrugged. 'I think Zach offended her by suggesting influencers were her thing. She thought he meant she was a featherhead only interested in her appearance.'

'I never said the wannabe fashion influencer was a featherhead,' said Marcus. 'She seems pretty savvy to me. It's possible she's part of something bigger, but that's by-the-by.'

'I also think that maybe when Zach first mentioned influencers and Nerys assumed he was talking about fashion, it hit a nerve.'

'Why?' said Marcus. 'Isn't she interested in clothes?'

'Yes, but she doesn't have much money. Plus little children tend to put their sticky hands on whatever you're wearing and ruin it. Unless you keep kids at arm's length, it's impossible to be glamorous. And Nerys is a hands-on mum.'

'How did you sort things out?'

'We talked things through. Once Nerys grasped that Zach really valued her ideas because she's more of the TikTok generation than I am – which made me feel a hundred years old – she said she'd see what she could find out and it might be worth a shot. I said "Let's do one thing at a time," and steered Zach back to improving my website and his college work. I said we'd look at the influencer thing later in the month. I *think* I've mollified both of them.'

'What does Dylan think?'

'I haven't told him yet. All he's talking about is a gig in a few weeks where his band is the support act. He's even hinting at asking for time off from the theatre to prepare.'

'When they're about to put on a big production?'

'He says it'll be more valuable for his A-level drama coursework, but he won't say how.' Fi leaned against Marcus and let him refill her glass. Below them, Hazeby's little dramas played out behind curtains and blinds. She felt like a mythical creature, wondering whether to cast a spell.

Where would she start?

Would she make Zach slow down enough that he wouldn't trip himself up, but at the same time wouldn't lose confidence? Make Nerys see how valuable she was and that she wasn't 'just a mum', but also a friend and a young woman with potential? Make Dylan work out his priorities? Show Marcus the missing pieces? Reassure Jade? She felt uneasy about Jade.

'Dylan talks to you more than Leo's ever talked to me,' said Marcus, interrupting her thoughts.

'They're different sorts of people.'

'That's true.' He hugged her. 'Come inside. There's rain in the air. I'll see how the gratin's doing, then we can spy on the other half of town from the front windows.'

The kitchen was full of rich aromas. In the oven, chicken bubbled in a savoury vegetable sauce under cheese-topped potatoes.

'Five more minutes,' he said. 'Shall we have the starter? It's little crab bites with chilli dipping sauce.'

Before Fi could answer, her phone vibrated. A message from her mother saying *Think how well you'd do here*, with a link. She sighed.

'What's wrong?' said Marcus, leaning over as she clicked. The link led to a website for an October apple festival in the Normandy village where her parents had a gîte complex. The website, in oranges, reds and golds, was delightful, with photographs of stalls heaped with apples and cheese, or displaying bottles of calvados and cider, and others full of local crafts and books. In the background, the wide river trickled under rich autumn-blue skies. It was suitable for a Dutch barge like *Coralie* to moor on, which was what her mother was hinting. Again.

'Looks great,' said Marcus. 'Another mini-break wouldn't go amiss. I'd better crack on with the case, then we can go.'

It would be nice to be away from all these fretting people, thought Fi, then heaved another sigh. It wouldn't work. She'd still be worrying about people and feeling guilty for leaving them to struggle. They'd been there for her a few months ago. 'Mmm,' she said.

'Mmm what? You keep saying you want me to meet your parents properly.'

'I do. But we've only just come back from a break.' She thought. 'Maybe we could go in November. After Hazeby Arts Festival is over and before I have to start gearing up for Christmas. There's too much going on at the moment. Too many people fretting. Zach, Nerys, Dylan and Jade. Not necessarily in that order.'

'I was going to ask about Jade,' said Marcus. 'She must be worried now that other shop has opened. I daresay you'd feel the same if it had been a chain bookshop.'

'Maybe.' Fi took the proffered plate of crab bites and sat at the dining table. 'I'd like to think it wouldn't be a problem, that we were serving different clients. There's a WH Smith's in town and that hasn't caused me any trouble. Nor did Mr Darcy's shop.'

'That was different.'

'I know.' Fi dipped her crab bite in the chilli sauce but didn't eat it. 'I keep telling Jade that she shouldn't worry. Magical Moments hasn't got any charm: all their stores are the same. There's a pattern they have to follow, stock they have to supply. Crystal Dreams is quite different.'

'But not as cheap.'

'Whose side are you on?'

Marcus held up his hands. 'Jade's, of course.'

'It doesn't sound like it.'

'There's room for both shops.'

Fi dipped the other side of the crab bite. 'Jade has crossed swords with the manager. The details are hazy, but I get the impression it was a bit snappy.'

'That's Jade being defensive,' said Marcus. 'As you say, Magical Moments is a store made with a cookie cutter: they're all identical. Its manager is probably the same – you could swap them with another branch manager and no one would even notice. Crystal Dreams and Jade are different. They're crafted from…'

'Magical wood? You're getting very poetic.'

Marcus chuckled. 'You know what I mean. There are bound to be people in town who want a bargain, and you can't stop that by wishful thinking. Either Jade has to find a way to compete or she should ride it out and stick to her guns, which has worked so far. Magical Moments is a novelty now. Before you know it, it won't be, and people will lose interest.'

'That's what I told her,' said Fi. 'In a week or two, most customers will realise that Jade offers something unique and if they've been lured away, they'll go back to her.'

'A lot of people after bargains probably buy online rather than from Crystal Dreams, anyway.'

'And tourists will prefer Jade's place because they're here to experience things and go to shops they can't elsewhere.'

'Exactly. Don't worry about Jade: things will work out. Come on, eat up. It took me hours to make those.'

'Did it?'

'Not really,' said Marcus. 'I bought them from Waitrose. Doing the main course wore me out.'

Fi grinned and glanced towards the window, beyond which stars twinkled and clouds drifted past.

All the same, she thought, *if I were a mythical creature looking down to perform magic, I'd start by putting Jade's mind at rest. It would be nice to see her relax for once.*

CHAPTER 5

Netta surveyed the shop as she came back from her lunch break. 'I brought you a coffee from Betsy's,' she said, holding out a tall cup.

'Thanks.' Jade accepted the cup, took off the lid and sipped the brew, which was just cool enough to drink.

'Still a bit quiet, then,' observed Netta.

Quiet? thought Jade. *It's dead.* 'It's always quiet on Wednesday afternoons,' she said.

'Is it? I hadn't noticed.' Netta pulled her laptop out of the counter drawer and opened it. Jade knew what would come next: an invitation to view average sales per hour, per day.

'So people are taking a look at Magical Moments this week,' said Jade. 'Of course they are. You'd expect that. You'd be a fool not to.'

'Uh huh.' Netta closed the laptop. 'How was

dinner with Rick?'

'So-so.'

In fact, her date with Rick the night before had been an unmitigated disaster. Unless, of course, storming out of a cosy candlelit dinner at your date's flat was how these things should work.

It had started so well. She had dressed up a bit, but not too much, and knocked on Rick's door ten fashionable minutes late. He had a nice bottle of red wine on standby and poured her a glass while he put the finishing touches to the lamb ragu. 'This has been simmering on low for three hours,' he said proudly. 'Fresh rigatoni to go with.'

'Wow,' said Jade. 'It smells lovely.'

'How was—'

'I don't want to talk about work.'

Rick raised his eyebrows. 'OK.' He continued stirring. 'What would you like to talk about?'

Jade shrugged. 'The state of the pop charts? Movie stars' diets? I don't mind.'

'Your call.' Rick got a fresh spoon and tasted the sauce. 'I'm sure it'll blow over.'

Jade tensed. 'What did I say?'

'I get that, but you're clearly worked up and I don't think you should be.' Rick put the tasting spoon in the sink and moved towards her. 'Shoulder rub?'

'I'm not stressed!' Jade snapped. 'I'm fine. Or rather, I would be fine if Magical flaming Moments and its flaming manager just disappeared.'

'That won't happen,' replied Rick. He was frowning, which was as close to angry as she'd ever seen him. 'Wishing the problem away won't solve it.'

Jade stared at him. 'One night off, that was all I wanted. But no, you had to stick your oar in.'

The pan on the stove started to bubble fiercely. Jade knew exactly how it felt. She put her wine glass on the worktop before she crushed it. 'I'm off.'

'Jade—'

'You don't know the half of it, Rick.' She got her coat from the hook on the back of the door and slammed her way downstairs.

The thought of going up to her flat next door and listening to Rick enjoying his solo supper didn't appeal one bit. Besides, he might try and patch things up with her and she wasn't in the mood. So Jade took herself to The Volunteer, an old man's pub at the other end of Hazeby which she'd never visited, drank two glasses of wine under the disapproving eyes of two men nursing pints, then found herself in the queue at the takeaway. At least they gave her what she wanted – a medium pepperoni with a side of onion rings – and didn't ask her about work.

Jade let herself in quietly, tiptoed upstairs, and took the pizza to bed with her, muttering about people who couldn't keep their mouths shut and other people who were out to get her. She woke at five am, sitting up in bed fully dressed and still clutching a crust of pizza. *Movie star diets*, she thought as she clambered into her pyjamas, which seemed to take a lot more effort than usual. *I bet Gwyneth Paltrow would have killed for that pizza.*

She was roused from her post-mortem of the previous evening by the sound of the shop door opening. She and Netta drew themselves up and stuck on smiles. 'Hello there,' said Mrs Brummell. 'I've come in for my echinacea. Nothing like it to keep colds at bay.'

'No problem,' said Jade. She came out from behind the counter and reached for the small bottle.

'The other shop doesn't have it, you know.'

Jade's hand froze in midair. 'You've been to Magical Moments, then?'

'Just to check it out. No offence, Jade: I've got to make my pension stretch as far as it can. You needn't worry, anyway. They've got some good deals, but they're not looking to attract people like me. And the shop didn't appeal.'

Jade brought the bottle to the counter. 'How do you mean, Mrs Brummell?'

Mrs Brummell tutted. 'My belief is that if you can't say anything nice, you shouldn't say anything at all.'

'Indeed,' said Jade, recalling the character assassination Mrs Brummell had performed on an old acquaintance not so long ago. Then again, it had helped her and Fi solve a murder case. 'Oh, I forgot to say – this is a pound off today. Snap discount.'

'Marvellous.' Mrs Brummell pulled out her purse. 'Yes, it's very bright and shiny and dare I say American, but it falls down on the service. The staff were more interested in chatting to each other than serving the customers. You should have seen the queue.'

'Oh dear,' said Jade. She closed her mouth firmly to keep from grinning.

'Like I said, don't worry,' said Mrs Brummell. 'I'm sure all the people who've gone over to them will come back soon enough.'

Jade managed to maintain a neutral expression while taking Mrs Brummell's payment and wishing her goodbye. As soon as the door had closed, she clutched at her hair. 'What are we going to do?'

'There's still the option of going big online,' said Netta. 'I've done a bit more social-media posting this week and we've got another twenty box subscribers. And don't forget this.' She opened the counter drawer.

Here we go again, thought Jade.

Netta pulled out a slim, full-colour A4 publication. On the front was a half-page photograph of her and Jade behind the counter of Crystal Dreams. The headline proclaimed: *SUBSCRIPTION BOXES AND AN ONLINE STORE WORK MAGIC FOR A RURAL*

BUSINESS. '*BizTech Retail News* think we're blazing our way towards the future.' She gazed at the photo fondly. 'Would you mind if I framed this and put it up in the shop?'

'Whatever,' said Jade. 'Right now, we don't have any customers to see it.'

'We do,' insisted Netta. 'They're growing. Online, anyway.'

'That's not what I mean and you know it.'

Netta's bottom lip pushed upwards and she looked away.

Jade sighed. 'Sorry, that came out wrong. What you've done is brilliant, Netta. I just feel sad about the work we've put in, only for some chain store to pinch our customers.'

Netta gave her a one-armed hug. 'Hopefully Mrs Brummell's right and they'll all come back.'

Jade managed a half smile. 'Maybe.'

'Course she is.' Netta paused. 'As it's quiet, would you mind if I went in the back and started putting together this month's boxes? We've got a few days, but I'd like to get going on it.'

'Sure,' said Jade. 'And sorry again for snapping. It isn't you. I'm a bit – stressed.'

'It's fine,' said Netta. 'I understand. If it does get busy later, give me a call. I can stop any time.'

The afternoon wore on, its long stretches punctuated by an occasional customer. All were regulars, and two-thirds of them – Jade kept a tally on the notepad – admitted they had visited the other shop. The feedback was that while everything was very competitively priced, it didn't have the atmosphere of Crystal Dreams.

'The staff seemed on edge,' said the first of the three witches. 'A tall man in a short-sleeved shirt was bobbing about and nudging them to get on with things, but they looked a bit lost.'

'Maybe they're new recruits who haven't been trained up yet,' said Jade.

'I don't think so,' said the first witch. 'I heard one of them say that they wished they hadn't moved over from the Wyvernton shop, and another one agreed.'

'Curiouser and curiouser,' said Jade, her smile lit by a warm internal glow.

'It was, rather,' said the first witch, 'and I didn't rate the quality. Now, my niece wants to improve her self-confidence. What would you recommend?'

At five o'clock, Jade decided that if no customers came in the next ten minutes, she would close early. She had spent the last half hour paging idly through *BizTech Retail News*, of which she had understood about half. She closed it and looked at the photo of herself and Netta beaming. *If we'd known then...*

That's a point – how's Netta getting on? I haven't heard a peep out of her.

In the back room, Netta was leaning over the table,

a dark-purple votive candle in each hand. The table was covered with smallish shallow boxes, stacked three deep. So was the worktop, and the seats of the two chairs. Two boxes had their lids open.

'How's it going?' asked Jade.

Netta slotted the candles into the open boxes. 'One-nine-eight, one-nine-nine,' she murmured. 'There.' She closed the lids and stepped back. 'Sorry, what did you say?'

'I asked how it was going,' said Jade.

'I've literally just finished.'

'Wow, well done!'

'Thanks,' said Netta, with a shy smile. 'I'll leave it till tomorrow to sort out collection, though. I'll take a picture or two to post on social media, then bin the packaging.' She waved a hand at an untidy heap of cardboard boxes and packing materials in the corner. 'There's plenty of room: it was only emptied on Monday.'

'Excellent,' said Jade. 'It's still quiet, so I'm closing early. We can resume the battle tomorrow. I'll cash up while you finish here.'

Netta gave her a thumbs up, then opened one of the boxes, turned her phone sideways and lined up the shot.

Maybe Netta's right, thought Jade. She went into the shop and opened the till, which revealed the day's small takings. *Maybe we should take the business online, but it wouldn't be the same*. She got bank bags from the drawer and began counting out pound coins.

'Seven, eight, nine, ten...' She surveyed what was left. It didn't look enough to fill the bag. Maybe the two-pound coins would be better.

She put the pound coins back in the till and took out a column of two-pound coins, weighing it in her hand. *Lots of people pay by card, anyway. Cash takings are only part of the story.* 'Two, four, six—'

Coins rolled over the counter as a scream rent the air. 'Netta!' cried Jade. 'Are you all right? What's happened?' She hurried into the back room.

Netta stumbled towards her, her face dead white. 'There's a – there's a body in the bin!'

'What?'

'There is! I saw it!'

For a moment, Jade let herself hope that an afternoon of staring at boxes and merchandise had made Netta's eyes go funny. Then she hurried outside to the big plastic bin.

It's too friendly, she found herself thinking, looking at its cheerful, chunky green plastic body. But she hesitated before lifting the lid.

She glanced inside, gasped, and dropped it.

'You saw,' said Netta. Her teeth were chattering. 'It's a body, isn't it?'

'Yes.' Jade took a deep breath and reopened the lid. A small woman was curled in the bottom of the bin as if asleep, but her eyes were wide and staring. She wore a dark coat, jeans and boots and her hair was half hidden by a black woollen hat. The only touch of colour was the scarf tied over her mouth and nose: white with red skulls on it. A scarf Jade sold in Crystal Dreams. 'We have to get her out, Netta. She might still be alive.'

'She doesn't look alive,' Netta choked out.

'Help me tip the bin. Then go and call an ambulance. And the police.'

Netta's hands shook so badly that Jade had to tip the bin by herself. The body flopped onto the wall of the bin. *It doesn't seem stiff,* thought Jade. *Hopefully that's good.*

Netta shrank back. 'Should you touch it? Isn't this a crime scene?'

'Yes, but if we can save her...' Jade tried to pull down the scarf but it kept catching on something. As she worked it free, she saw leaves and stems. The woman's mouth had been stuffed with— 'Is that thyme?' She pulled out as much as she could and felt for a pulse. Nothing. She put her hand over the woman's mouth. Was that a faint breath, or not? 'I'm not sure she's alive either, Netta, but phone for an ambulance and the police. Please.'

But Netta was rooted to the spot. 'It's her, isn't it?'

Jade had been so busy trying to save the woman that she had paid no attention to her face. She looked again and Linzi Lawson stared back at her with glazed eyes, her mouth open in a silent, horrified scream.

CHAPTER 6

'OK, breathe.' Fi wasn't sure if she was talking to herself or Jade. Her own heart was hammering so hard she could barely hear. 'You think she's still alive?'

'I cleared her airway and I *thought* maybe she was breathing. We started doing chest compressions, but…'

'You've dialled 999?'

'Yes, of course. Police and ambulance. The controller said the emergency services would go to the front of the shop, but that doesn't make sense. The bin's out back and the alley has plenty of room… I don't want them turning up where the whole town can see.'

'The 999 call centre is in the next county,' said Fi, in what she hoped was a soothing voice. 'The controller probably doesn't know the town, but the emergency services will. Don't worry, they'll work it out.'

'Can you come? Netta's in a state. She's never seen a— I can't say it. Maybe it isn't one. But it's Linzi Lawson. I don't like her but I wouldn't wish this on anyone... Please come. Use the alley and knock on the back gate and I'll let you in. I don't want half the world seeing you turn up, either.'

'Jade, I come round all the time. No one will even notice. Try and calm down. I'll be there as soon as I can.'

Dylan looked out of his cabin. 'What's going on?'

'Someone's fallen ill at Crystal Dreams,' said Fi. 'Can you help Zach in the shop?'

'I'm doing homework.'

'No you're not. You're listening to music and messaging your friends. Go and help. I shan't be long.'

Never mind Netta being in a state: Jade didn't sound much better. Fi needed to hurry, and cycling would be quicker than running. She collected her bike from the store and swerved round pedestrians and cars in exactly the way she always told Dylan not to.

She paused at the end of the alley which led to the rear of Crystal Dreams. The light was failing, but she could make out the gate to Jade's yard. She waited for Jade to peer out but it stayed closed. There was no sign of an emergency vehicle. Perhaps the police had arrived on foot.

Fi was about to cycle down the alley when she realised that her earlier reassurance to Jade made no sense. Yes, the 999 control centre was in the next county, but that didn't mean they wouldn't know the details of the streets in Hazeby-on-Wyvern. They'd look up Jade's address to send the emergency services to the right place. If Jade said the bin was at the back, they'd know there was an access alley.

So if the controller had told Jade the ambulance crew would come to the front, there must be a reason. And it was pretty obvious what that reason was.

Even from the little Jade had stammered out, the police would want the alley left as undisturbed as possible so that they could hunt for clues. It was surprising there wasn't already tape across it. Fi might only confuse matters. Her sense of discomfort increasing, she made her way to the front door.

The sign was turned to *Closed* and the lights in the main shop were off. She locked up her bike, then rapped on the door and waited. In no time, Jade let her in.

'Are the police here yet?' Fi whispered.

'No, and I said to come round the back,' Jade muttered, as she ushered Fi forward.

'I didn't want to leave tyre tracks or footprints down there. It may be a crime scene. No one falls into a bin in a private yard. I mean, people sometimes climb into them in public places when they're very drunk or skip-diving or hiding from someone. They don't seek them in locked yards. The police will need to gather evidence. They probably don't want things churned up by the ambulance, either, which is why that's been told to come to the front. Or did I miss something? Could it be a really weird accident?'

Jade stopped. 'I— I don't think so: I thought maybe a suicide attempt. But could you suffocate yourself? Wouldn't instinct make you pull out the herbs?'

'Herbs?'

'In her mouth. Didn't I tell you? I took them out to help her breathe, but now I think it was just my imagination that she was breathing at all.'

'No pulse?'

'Not that I can tell. She's ice cold, but it's not warm out – and if she's in shock that might make a difference – but... I tried chest compressions but neither of us is sure I was doing it right. Maybe it was pointless, but I couldn't—'

Someone hammered at the front door and they saw two people in green peering through the glass. Beyond them loomed an ambulance. Jade hurried to let them in.

'Hi,' said the first woman as she entered. 'I'm Davina, lead paramedic, and this is Karen. You're Jade, is that right? And, er . . . you're Netta?'

'Netta's with the . . . the casualty,' said Jade. 'This is my friend Fi. She's come to help.'

'We met last December, didn't we?' Karen, hefting a backpack big enough for a parachute, gave a friendly smile. 'At least we can see what we're doing this time and it's not so cold.'

'Just to let you know, we have body cameras,' said Davina, tapping a device attached to her uniform.

'I thought you only used those when you anticipated trouble,' said Fi, baffled. What did they think Jade or Netta would do?

'Not always,' said Davina. 'The police are delayed and I understand this may be a crime scene, so they've asked us to record everything we can. Body cam is the best we can do. Where's the casualty?'

'Through here,' said Jade, as they hurried towards the back of the shop. 'We tipped the bin to get her to a position where we could help her breathe. She had herbs in her mouth. I thought I could feel a breath and I did chest compressions, but…'

'Thank you, Jade.' Davina patted her shoulder. 'You can stand down. Karen's got the crash kit. If there's anything more to be done, we'll do it. This way?'

In the yard, Netta was on her haunches next to the tipped bin. Her shoulders were shaking.

Karen crouched beside her. 'Don't cry, love,' she said. 'Go inside. We'll take over. You and Jade have done all you could.'

Netta joined Fi and Jade in the doorway. Jade put an arm round Netta, who rested her head on Jade's shoulder, her sobs subsiding.

It was now dark. The yard was lit only by the small light over the back door and the coloured bulbs that Rick had strung across it months before. The little lights on the paramedics' body cams twinkled incongruously as they moved about the scene, muttering.

'Why aren't they saving her?' whispered Netta. But the question sounded flat, as if she was asking for the sake of it. There was no answer to give. From where they stood, even in the dusk, it was obvious that Linzi Lawson was beyond saving.

After what seemed like a century, the two paramedics carefully examined her. Linzi's legs were still tucked up as if she was sleeping. Checks, tests, torchlight shone in her face and down her body. The crash kit remained untouched. After another century, Karen sat back on her heels and Davina came over to Jade.

'If it's any consolation, there was nothing you could have done to save her,' she said. 'It's for the coroner to decide, of course, but from everything we can observe, the woman has been dead for a good many hours: at a guess, a bit under twenty-four. The forensic pathologist will need to do tests to get a better idea. Rigor mortis has largely worn off in the upper part of her body, which is why you thought she might still be alive, but it hasn't gone completely from her legs and lower body. The police will ask how she was lying when you found her. I don't suppose either of you took a photograph?'

Jade shook her head. Netta made a retching sound, pulled away from Jade and rushed inside.

'Sorry,' said Davina. 'You'd best get a cup of tea or something. I'll move the ambulance round the corner before the local gossips start gathering, then radio to see what's keeping the police and what they want us to do next. I'll tell the police to park discreetly and suggest they seal off the alley. Inspector Falconer doesn't usually take offence at my suggestions, unlike some.'

'I'll open the gate for you,' said Jade, as if she was on autopilot.

As Davina left through the shop, Fi followed Jade. They paused on the doorstep. Under the pretty lights, the covered form of Linzi Lawson looked tiny and indistinguishable as human. Beyond, the gate to the alley was barely visible in the shadows.

A cat appeared from nowhere and padded along the top of the fence, triggering the security light. Jade gasped.

'What?' whispered Fi.

'The gate's unbolted.'

Fi peered: Jade was right. Rick had painted the bolt mauve to tone in with the colours around the yard. It was slightly luminous in the security light, and clearly drawn back.

'So what? Weren't you about to put the bins out?'

'No,' said Jade. 'They went out on Monday. The last time I unbolted it was… I'm not entirely sure, but not for a day or so. This is just too weird. Where's Marcus?'

'I don't know. Let's go in: I'll message him.'

'The signal's rubbish here.'

'Then I'll go to the front.'

They went into the main shop, passing displays that seemed poised to listen.

Where are you? Fi typed, and pressed *Send*.

Jade gasped.

Fi looked up. Davina had underestimated the ability of the gossips of Hazeby to sniff out trouble. A small group of people had gathered in the street and were pressing their noses against the glass.

As the ambulance slowly pulled away, blue lights appeared above the heads of the gawpers. With a squeal of brakes, something stopped outside Crystal Dreams.

'Thank goodness,' Fi whispered, as her phone vibrated.

I'm in Spetisham on the case, Marcus messaged. *I'll call later if I can. What's up?*

'I've never been so glad to see Marcus,' said Jade.

'It isn't Marcus.'

'Then who—'

The gawpers on the pavement parted like the Red Sea and the front door of Crystal Dreams swung open.

'Jade Fitch,' said Inspector Nina Acaster. 'Whatever have you done *this* time?'

CHAPTER 7

'It wasn't me,' Jade said automatically. She could have kicked herself.

She heard the door of the staff bathroom click. Netta came in, saw Nina, and gasped.

'It's all right, Netta,' said Jade. 'Inspector Acaster is here to ask a few questions and manage the investigation.' She felt slightly comforted that someone in the room was more scared than she was. Though whether Netta had reason to be was another matter entirely.

'Thank you, Jade,' said Nina. 'If I might continue?' Her suit was as smart as ever and her blonde crop as precise, but she seemed a fraction less sharp. Still a precision instrument, but less likely to take your arm off just by looking at you. 'Can one of you fill me in briefly on what's happened tonight?'

'Netta found a body in my wheelie bin,' said Jade.

'We tried to save her, but the paramedics think she's been dead for nearly twenty-four hours.'

'OK,' said Nina. She pulled a black notebook from her pocket, slid a matching pen with silver bands from the clip that held it, and clicked it on. 'Who was present when the body was found?'

'Netta and me,' said Jade. 'Once we'd phoned for an ambulance and the police, I rang Fi and asked if she could come round.'

'Netta hasn't seen a body before,' said Fi, 'and understandably, she's shaken. Would it be possible for her to give her statement later? Perhaps at home?'

'No!' Netta cried. 'I live with my parents, and they—' She swallowed. 'I'd rather do it now.'

'As you wish.' Nina found a fresh page in her notebook. 'Let's start with the easy bit. Can you give me your name and address, please.'

'Viennetta Louise Brown,' Netta gabbled. To her credit, Nina didn't flinch. 'My address is 10 Rycroft Gardens, Hazeby-on-Wyvern, Wyvernshire. Do you want my postcode?'

'No thanks.' Nina finished writing. 'I assume you prefer Netta.'

'Yes.' Netta's cheeks were flushed.

'OK, Netta, in your own words, can you tell me how you came to discover the – Ms Lawson?'

'I was putting together subscription boxes,' said Netta.

'Subscription boxes?'

'For the shop. They're small boxes with a selection of items that we post out to our box subscribers once a month. The back room's covered in them.'

'Ah.'

'So I finished filling them as Jade came through to see how I was doing, and she said she was thinking of closing early so I said I'd take the empty packaging out to the bin—'

'Wait a moment.' Nina looked up from the notepad. 'Can you remember what time that was?'

'After five, definitely. So I gathered up as much packaging as I could carry and took it outside, and when I opened the big green bin there was… I ran in. No, I screamed, then ran in and told Jade and she came out. She said we had to get the – the person out in case they were still alive, so she did and she told me to phone the ambulance and the police but I couldn't move. So she pulled down the scarf and took out the herbs and then she rang.'

'Did you touch the body at any time?'

Netta shook her head vigorously.

'Apart from lifting the bin lid when you opened it, did you touch the bin any further?'

'No. I wanted to help, but – I think I was in shock.'

'I'm not surprised,' said Nina. 'This isn't the sort of thing that happens every day.' Her glance flicked towards Jade. 'Well, not to you.' She reread what she had written. 'Before this evening, can you remember the last time you put anything in the bin or handled it?'

Netta thought. 'It was emptied on Monday. That morning, I flattened a couple of cardboard boxes and put them in.'

'OK, that'll do. If you like, you can read what I've written and tell me if it's correct.' She held out her notebook to Netta, who took it, scanned it and handed it back with a nod. 'Can I have your phone number, in case I need to contact you?'

Netta recited it so fast that Nina had to ask her to repeat it.

'You're free to go, Netta, but can I ask you not to discuss this with anyone. You can tell your parents, of course, but please ask them not to discuss it more widely.'

'I will. Thank you.' Netta fetched her bag and coat. 'I – I'm sorry I was a bit wobbly.'

'You did very well, Netta.'

So this is what she's like when she doesn't have it in for you, thought Jade, and chided herself for being uncharitable. It wasn't Netta's fault she'd got caught up in whatever this was.

'Netta, if you don't feel up to coming in tomorrow, that's fine,' she said. 'Just text.'

Netta managed a wavering smile. 'Bye, Jade. Bye, Fi.'

'Are you OK walking home?' asked Fi. 'We could phone you a taxi.'

'It's only ten minutes away, I'll be fine.' Netta hurried out. *I understand Fi's concern*, thought Jade. *But let's face it, the danger's in here, not in the town.*

She turned to Nina, who was observing her with a neutral expression. Jade hoped it didn't mean the same as Marcus Falconer's neutral expression, which she distrusted intensely. 'I suppose it's me next,' she said.

'If you don't mind.'

'Would you like a drink? Cup of tea? Water?'

'I'm fine, thanks. You can have one if you want.'

'I can make one,' said Fi. 'If that's OK.'

'Whatever,' said Nina. She turned to Jade. 'We'll take name and address as read. In your own words, can you tell me about the events leading up to the discovery of the body?'

'Before you begin,' said Fi, 'tea or coffee, Jade?'

'Tea, please,' said Jade. 'Nice and strong.'

'Of course,' said Fi, and went into the back room.

Jade marshalled her thoughts, which wasn't helped by various tea-making noises from the back room. Somehow, it reminded her of sound effects in a play on the radio. 'How far back should I go?'

'As far as necessary.'

'OK. Netta went into the back room to do the boxes mid-afternoon. They don't need posting yet, but she likes to start them early. Netta's been working hard on growing the subscription side of the business. I said I'd call her if it got busy in the shop, but it didn't.'

'So Netta was on her own in the back room from mid to late afternoon. Can you remember what time you went through to her?'

'It had turned five. Because it was quiet, I decided that if we didn't have any more customers in the next ten minutes I'd close early. Then I went through to see how Netta was doing.'

'So just after five. Say five past?'

'About that. Netta was finishing the last two boxes and she said she'd take the packaging out. I went through to the main shop and began to cash up. I'd been doing that for maybe a couple of minutes when Netta screamed. I rushed in and she told me she'd seen a body. I went out, she followed. I opened the bin and there it was.'

Nina leaned forward. 'Can you describe what you saw?'

'A small woman curled up at the bottom of the bin. She was in black, except for a white scarf with red skulls tied over the lower half of her face. Her eyes were open. I tipped the bin to get her out and worked the scarf loose. There were herbs stuffed in her mouth, which I took out. All that time, I was telling Netta to phone for an ambulance and the police—'

'In that order?'

'Yes, in that order. She was rooted to the spot, so in the end I did it.'

'Did you think the woman was still alive?'

What's the right answer? Is there a right answer? 'I wasn't sure,' Jade said, eventually. 'I hoped she was. I checked for a pulse and couldn't find one. I couldn't tell if she was still breathing. I tried doing chest compressions but it didn't work.' She shivered. 'I'm doing a CPR course, after this.'

'That's probably a good idea,' said Nina.

What's that supposed to mean?

'And then…?' Nina prompted.

'Then I rang Fi and asked if she could come over. To be honest, I felt as if I could do with some help supporting Netta. I wasn't sure how she'd hold up to being questioned.'

'Quite.' Nina finished writing and looked up. 'Couple more questions. Did Netta go outside at all this afternoon, before she went out and found the body?'

'She would have done, to get stock for the boxes. I heard the door open once, and again a few minutes later. That would be Netta going to the shed and coming back. I don't think I heard anything apart from that. That was mid-afternoon, probably just after she first went through. I can't say a definite time.'

'Uh huh. Did you know who the body was?'

Jade's mouth was dry. Fi came through with the tea. 'Sorry about that: the kettle took a while. I've used the tea towel to handle most things – kettle, door and drawer handles – in case you want to take prints.' She gave Jade a mug and moved a few steps away with her own drink.

Jade sipped the tea gratefully. 'Yes, I did know who she was – but not until I'd got the scarf and herbs out of the way. She was curled up in the bin and her hair was under a hat. Netta recognised her first.'

'How did Netta know who she was?' Nina's pen was poised above the paper.

'She came to the shop a few days ago, just before her own shop was due to open. She's – she was the manager of the new Magical Moments shop. I caught her casing the joint and taking notes: she was clearly here to snoop.' Jade took another sip of her tea. *You should tell her. Get it over with.*

But what if—

'We had words in the shop that day,' she said, before she had a chance to change her mind. 'I knew who she was because I'd been on the company website researching this rival shop. She had the cheek to offer me a deal where her shop would do what it was good at and I'd get the scraps, more or less. So I told her no deal. In fact, what I actually said was that, as far as I was concerned, this meant war.' She paused, and no one said anything to fill the silence.

'The customers in the shop can probably confirm that, and Netta was there too.'

Nina's immaculate eyebrows looked as if they might never return to their usual place. 'Were you worried about the new shop?'

'I was,' said Jade. 'I've worked hard to build up this business. Having a chain come in who can undercut me on price – obviously it's not ideal. I've definitely lost trade since Magical Moments opened, though I've had customers tell me it doesn't have the atmosphere of this place.' She waved a hand at the shelves, the midnight-blue walls, the silver stars. 'I'm fully aware that this doesn't look good. What's more, I was supposed to be having dinner with my – with Rick yesterday evening and I walked out because he started talking about shop stuff. I went to the Volunteer and had a couple of drinks, then went for a pizza and took it home.' *You may as well slap the cuffs on now*, she thought, and sighed.

'Can you remember when you left Rick's – house? Flat?'

'It's a flat, next door to mine. He rents that and the shop underneath.'

'Rick Jennings?'

'That's him.'

'Any idea when you left there?'

'I was meant to be there at seven thirty. I was a bit late, so twenty to eight. I don't think I was there more than ten minutes.'

'Ten to eight,' said Nina, making a note.

'Then I walked across town to the Volunteer. That took maybe fifteen minutes. Yes, because the clock on the wall said ten past eight when I sat down with a drink. I had two glasses of wine, got a pizza from Luigi's and went home. I'm pretty sure I was asleep by ten.'

'We'll check with the pub and the takeaway,' said Nina. 'Anything else to add?'

'What about the bolt, Jade?' said Fi.

'Oh gosh, yes. Thanks, I'd nearly forgotten. I went to open the gate for the paramedics, but the bolt was already drawn.'

'So anyone could have walked into your yard, basically,' said Nina. 'Is that normal?'

'No, not at all. I mean, the sheds have padlocks, so it's not the end of the world if the gate isn't bolted, but it always would be. Unless one of us forgot to bolt it when we brought in the bin on Monday.'

'Which of you did that?'

'Netta. I popped out for something and when I got in she told me she'd done it.'

'Did you go into the yard between the bin coming back and this evening?'

'No. I'd usually be in and out for stock, but as I said, it was quiet.'

'OK.' Nina paused. 'Thank you for being honest

about your previous contact with Ms Lawson and your movements last night. That's saved us a lot of time and potential trouble, and I appreciate it can't have been easy.'

Jade nodded, not trusting herself to speak.

'If you want to read my notes, you may.'

Jade held out a hand for the notebook and skimmed Nina's notes. They were organised, with bullet points, and written in rounded characters with small up and down strokes. They were nothing like Jade would have imagined. 'That's fine.'

'Fi, as I gather you weren't involved until after the discovery of the body, I'll pay you a visit at a later date. Unless there's something you wish to add?'

'I've nothing to add,' said Fi. 'Is it all right if Jade comes back to the boat with me tonight? I expect you'll be busy here.'

Nina half smiled. 'I must admit I was hoping you'd offer.' She turned to Jade. 'I assume you're happy with that. Same mobile number?'

Jade nodded. 'I'll pack a bag,' she managed to say, and somehow got to the door which led to her flat. She climbed the stairs slowly, clutching the handrail, then let herself in and stuffed a couple of changes of clothes, pyjamas and toiletries in a large bag. She remembered her phone charger as she was heading out, and returned for it.

'Got everything?' said Nina. 'I'll give you a call

when you can come back, but I warn you that it may take some time, depending on what we find.'

'The spare keys are in the counter drawer,' said Jade. She paused. 'Thanks for not shouting at me.'

Nina opened the drawer. 'These ones?' she said, holding up a white rubber skull with a few keys dangling from it.

'That's right.'

'We'll get going,' said Fi.

Jade let Fi leave first, then pulled the door to behind her. It felt strange not to lock it. At least the crowd had dispersed, though people were still gawping as they passed.

'You did the right thing,' said Fi, as they walked along, Fi wheeling her bike. 'It must have been hard.'

'It was,' said Jade. *But not as bad as Nina Acaster being nice to me. Sure, she was nice to Netta too, but Netta's young and she was scared. Was she nice to me because she thinks I'll be convicted? Because there's no hope for me? Looking at the facts, I have to be the number one suspect.* And Jade tortured herself with thoughts of arrest, cross-examination and prison all the way to the Book Barge.

CHAPTER 8

The Book Barge was welcoming. Warm light glowed through the curtains and spilled onto the grass. Stan ran up as soon as Fi opened the wheelhouse door and snuffled round their legs, his tail wagging in greeting.

Dylan was less welcoming: friendly to Jade but giving his mother the side-eye.

I don't have time for this, thought Fi, but smiled as brightly as she could manage. 'Thanks for helping Zach and closing up. Sorry I was longer than I intended. Jade's staying over and I'm ordering a Chinese takeaway. What do you fancy?'

Dylan's expression darkened further. What had happened in the time she'd been away? A difficult customer? A shoplifter? He swallowed. 'Aren't you going out with Carla?' It sounded like an accusation.

'Oh,' said Jade, hunched in her coat, her anxiety making even that one syllable wobble. 'I didn't realise. I can stay at the Crown or something.'

'Don't worry, Jade, we postponed it yesterday,' said Fi. 'Even if we hadn't, you could still have stayed here.' She extracted a storage bag from the airing cupboard in the private quarters. 'Here's the bedding for the sofa bed in the aft. Do you want help?'

'No, I'm fine. I've done it often enough.'

'OK.' Fi gave her a quick hug. 'By the time you've got things set up and maybe messaged Rick, I'll have found a bottle of wine and the takeaway menu.'

She waited until Jade had pulled the curtain separating the aft section from the main part, then turned to Dylan. 'I told you Carla cancelled yesterday,' she whispered. 'Why are you snapping at me?' She knew she was snapping too, but she was tired. She wished, not for the first time, that there was more space on the boat so that she could talk to Jade in peace. On the other hand, perhaps it was better for Jade to be distracted by someone else's family life. Even if the distraction would be bickering.

'I'm not, and I can't remember everything,' said Dylan. 'I thought I'd have the boat to myself this evening.'

Fi looked around her. In the evenings, the main part of the bookshop was their sitting room, the sofa set up to face a large TV hidden by a panel during the day. Now, the sofa was pushed back and some of the display tables on lockable wheels had been moved so that two armchairs could be brought forward.

She drew Dylan into the galley. 'How many people did you plan to have round without asking?'

'Only five, and I *did* ask. You weren't listening.'

'Five? Who?'

'Alfie, Max, Chloe, Livvy and Ruby. Chloe will be here any minute, and the rest are coming in half an hour.'

'You definitely didn't tell me that. That's basically a party. Apart from anything else, it's a school night. Please don't pretend you'll all be doing homework together. I was your age once.'

'We'll be gaming,' whispered Dylan, with as much dignity as he could manage under the circumstances. 'We're allowed time off. It's still the autumn term and we don't have much homework. Livvy and Max are at college and don't have *any*. *And* you were going to be out. This is my home too. It's not my fault your friends are flaky and always standing you up or having a crisis and we don't have room to swing a cat.'

'Rrrerrfff?' woofed Stan, sniffing the air and peering under the table for possible feline visitors.

Fi and Dylan glared at each other. From behind the curtain at the other end of the boat came the sound of Jade battling with the sofa bed. At least that would keep her busy for a while. Hopefully she'd message Rick, and maybe he would come round and help comfort her. Whatever their row had been about, it would blow over if Rick had anything to do with it. He was too laidback to hold grudges. Although maybe Nina was questioning him and he wouldn't be able to come.

Fi was on the verge of telling Dylan to cancel his plans. She could sense him waiting for her to do it: his arms were folded, his jaw clenched, his cheeks flushed. But he would feel humiliated and angry if he had to tell his friends they couldn't come round after all. Perhaps he'd storm off with them to somewhere less safe.

And there might be an advantage to their coming. The teenagers would be too busy with each other to listen to Fi and Jade talking, whereas if Dylan were there on his own, he'd hear everything.

Fi considered. She didn't know Livvy and Ruby, but Dylan and his friends seemed to attract the quieter sort of girl. Hopefully they were too shy for anything more than a little kissing between games, if that had even been part of the intention. Maybe they'd intended to raid the few alcoholic drinks in the cupboard, but they wouldn't get to raid it now and they probably wouldn't be kissing either. They'd have to settle for killing zombies or racing cars.

'Fine,' she said. 'I'll get food from the Chinese – not masses, mind – but you'll stay in here gaming, and I *mean* gaming. Jade and I will stay in the kitchen, and everyone goes home at nine. If anyone brings alcohol, they all leave and you're grounded for a month. Deal?'

Dylan's tension eased and he almost smiled. 'Nine thirty?'

'Nine thirty. On the dot.'

'Deal. But don't fuss: it's not fair.' Dylan started messaging on his phone. 'What's up with Jade, anyway?'

'She's got a lot going on and needs a bit of TLC.' It felt dishonest not explaining about Linzi, but Fi didn't know exactly how, or how to deal with the response. She knew what Dylan would say, because it was going through her own head. *Not again. How can so many dead bodies happen to two ordinary people? Why can't either of us catch a break?*

Jade walked in. Dylan lifted his head and smiled more naturally. 'I guess Magical Moments is causing you grief at the moment, but you shouldn't worry,' he said. 'We all prefer Crystal Dreams. It's got a better vibe, and your stuff isn't plastic tat. It's better for the environment.'

Jade blinked. 'I hadn't even thought of that.'

'Your generation doesn't,' said Dylan, finishing his message with a final stab of his forefinger. 'You don't always know what's important. You should get Netta to put up a poster saying so.'

Jade flopped down in a chair and Stan jumped in

her lap for his ears to be scratched.

Fi sat opposite with the takeaway menu.

There was a knock on the wheelhouse door.

'That'll be Chloe,' Dylan dashed through the boat. 'You and Mum will have to entertain each other, I'm afraid.'

'I think entertainment might be pushing it,' said Jade, but Dylan had gone.

Within half an hour, the main part of the boat was full of laughter and chatter. If Dylan's friends were annoyed about chaperones behind a thin door, it was largely countered by a mass of food to share. To be fair, they were a good bunch.

Fi and Jade sat in the galley nursing glasses of wine. Jade hadn't eaten a great deal, but periodically nibbled at a prawn cracker. They'd talked over what had happened from top to bottom and back again, but it hadn't helped.

'Why me?' said Jade, for the hundredth time. 'Why my shop? Why didn't I stay at Rick's? What will Hugo say? Why can't I have a quiet life? What did I ever do to the universe? Why was Nina so nice? And why Nina?'

'Because Marcus is on another case,' said Fi, for the hundredth time.

That was the only question that was easy to answer. Marcus had messaged shortly after they arrived at the boat. *Just heard. Can't get involved though. Busy on this case and division decided Nina was best in circs. Do the right thing – both of you. Don't interfere.*

It's nothing to do with Jade, she'd messaged back. *She rang it in straight away. We ARE doing the right thing.*

I still can't take the case on. Lunch tomorrow?

Fi didn't know what else to say, and he hadn't messaged again. She knew he was on a tricky case, and doubtless his division head had determined that Marcus couldn't be involved in any case relating to Fi and Jade. Not that they'd expected that to be an issue – who would? It irritated her, all the same. Couldn't he ring? Was 'can't get involved' the best response he could think of? Jade was his friend too. Couldn't he understand how she must be feeling?

'What Dylan said about plastic tat and so on,' said Jade. 'I wonder…'

'Yes?' Fi felt a sense of relief that perhaps Jade was finally coming out of her loop of negative thoughts.

'I wonder if those herbs in Linzi's mouth were there to say "this is from a proper witch shop". It's worse than I thought. I'm not even sure what herbs they were. I only use them in cooking. Not those ones. I mean dried ones in little tubs from the supermarket.'

Fi put her hand over Jade's. 'Stop it: you'll drive yourself insane. Nina was quite reasonable when she was questioning you, so she can't think you've got anything to do with this. She's just getting a picture. No one could imagine you suffocating someone: it's too horrible. You're not a horrible person.'

'I must be, for this to keep happening.'

'Life isn't like that,' said Fi. 'Sometimes things go wrong. This is one of those times.'

'You sound like an inspirational poster,' snapped Jade.

I'm trying to help, thought Fi, biting back words that would make things worse. Her phone pinged with a message – but it was from her mother, not Marcus. She pushed the phone about the table but didn't pick it up.

The galley door burst open and Dylan peered round. 'You two look as miserable as cats in a cold bath. I've made you an avatar, Jade. It's got mad purple hair, a lime-green dress and sparkly blue shades. Come and do some racing, that'll cheer you up.'

For the first time in days, Jade managed a weak smile. 'Maybe you're right. I could do with winning at something. But I'm sorting that avatar out first.' She got up.

'I'll stay here for a bit,' said Fi. She picked up the phone and opened her mother's message.

Have you thought any more about coming to the cider festival? I won't push you, but the pace of life is so much calmer. You could do with a break.

The message was accompanied by a photograph of that other river, flowing under golden-leaved trees, waiting for a new boat to moor up.

Fi put the phone face down. Jade's words hurt, along with Marcus's and Dylan's. *Don't fuss. This is my home too. Don't interfere. You sound like an inspirational poster.* She couldn't do anything right for anyone. For the first time, running away to France actually appealed.

CHAPTER 9

Jade woke with a start, yet again. It was still dark. She registered that she wasn't in her own bed and froze. But the bedlinen wasn't the scratchy blanket she would expect in a prison bunk, and the bed was fairly comfortable. She felt under the pillow, found her phone, and shone the torch around the book-lined walls. 'You're at Fi's,' she whispered. 'You're at Fi's, and you're safe.'

This was, what, the fifth time she had woken? Every time, she had panicked. Once she had heard a loud clang and assumed it was someone shutting her in. It had taken her heartbeat a few minutes to return to normal. She checked her phone: 5.29 am. 'Please let me sleep,' she whispered, to any being that would listen, and buried herself beneath the covers.

The next time she woke, the Book Barge was coming to life. Dylan was grumbling about something, while Fi sounded as if she was reasoning with him. A chair scraped. Light peeped round the edges of the curtain dividing her sleeping area from the rest of the boat. *Time to face the day*, thought Jade, and suppressed a groan.

She forced herself out of bed and padded into the living area. The door to Fi and Dylan's quarters was open: they were sitting at the galley table. A normal domestic scene.

Fi looked round. 'Morning, Jade. Sleep OK?'

'Not bad.' There was no point in describing her various nightmares or the seemingly endless stretches of time she had spent awake in the night, scrolling through the news and social media for any mention of what had happened. At least she had found nothing except minor speculation on the local Facebook group. She yawned. Then her phone buzzed.

A message from Netta: *Dear Jade, I won't be coming into work today. Hope that's OK. I can still do online stuff at home, so I'll get on with that. Hope you're feeling all right. Sorry – Netta.*

Jade put the phone in her pyjama pocket. 'Netta won't be in today. Probably for the best, since I doubt I'll be opening.'

'Oh yeah?' said Dylan, reaching for another piece of toast.

'That's your fourth,' said Fi. 'Leave some for Jade, please.' She looked – not terrible, but as if she hadn't slept well either. There were faint purple smudges under her eyes, and the fine lines around her mouth were easier to see.

'There is some!' said Dylan, his voice rising with the injustice of it. 'There's two pieces left.'

Fi sighed. 'Tea or coffee, Jade?'

'Tea. Don't get up, I can make it.' Jade switched on the kettle and got herself a mug. 'Anyone want a refill?'

Dylan held out his mug. 'Please. Tea, loads of milk.'

'Uh huh.'

Jade was filling Dylan's mug when her phone buzzed in her pocket. Not a text, but a call. She put water in her own mug and set the kettle down before retrieving it.

The display said *Scary Nina*.

'It's her,' said Jade, 'she's ringing me.' She stared at Fi. 'What do I do?'

'You answer it,' said Fi. 'Don't worry, it'll be fine.'

'I wish I had your optimism,' Jade replied. *Then again, if she was going to arrest me, she wouldn't make a courtesy call first. She'd come round and do it.* She pressed *Answer*. 'Hello?'

'Good morning,' said Nina. 'Just a quick call to say that our teams have finished with your shop, so you can go back in when you're ready.'

'Really?'

'Yes. We've done all we need to. We've dusted for prints – mostly outside, but some door handles and surfaces in the back room and the shop – and we've taken photos. Oh, and we've taken a couple of things for examination.'

'What things?' asked Jade, panic rising so fast that she thought she might be sick.

'Nothing much. One of your skull scarves and a couple of samples of herbs, for comparison purposes. And no, that doesn't mean I'm planning to come round and arrest you. For one thing, no knives on your premises fit the wound.'

'What wound?'

'The one in the victim's back,' said Nina. 'No way you could have seen it: the coat covered it completely. Whatever the murderer used, they took with them.'

'So you're treating it as murder,' said Jade.

'Well, yes. Unless Linzi Lawson was a contortionist, there's no way she could have stabbed herself there, never mind the rest of it. The herbs and the scarf were either window dressing or just making sure. The murderer was lucky: it looks as if the stab wound stopped her heart immediately. If it hadn't, there would have been a lot of blood. Maybe the murderer didn't know that, and hoped the herbs would choke her if the stabbing didn't do the trick. We'll have to wait on the results of the post-mortem for any finer detail. Sorry, I hope you aren't eating breakfast.'

'I won't be,' said Jade. Even the thought of picking up a butter knife made her queasy. 'I doubt I'll open today.'

'Mmm. Maybe you should. If you're closed, people will put two and two together and make fifteen, and you don't want that. But it's up to you.'

'OK. Thanks, Nina.'

'You should address me as Inspector Acaster,' said Nina.

That made Jade feel better. 'Sorry, Inspector Acaster.'

'I'll let you get on,' said Nina, and rang off.

Fi and Dylan were watching her. Dylan's eyes were like saucers. 'So it's a murder?' he said. 'Another one?'

'Yes, another one,' said Jade. 'And no, you can't tell anyone or drop any hints.'

'I know how to behave,' said Dylan. 'Wait a minute, I heard you say "wound". Was it a stabbing?'

'You'll get nothing out of me,' said Jade. 'I should have left the room when I saw who the call was from. Sorry, Fi.'

'You should be on your way to school, Dylan,' said Fi.

Dylan looked at his watch. 'I've got ages yet. Now I'm in sixth form, no one cares if you're a bit late.'

'I care, and I want to talk to Jade. So off you go.'

Dylan crammed the rest of his slice of toast in his

mouth, finished making his tea and took it to his room, muttering about missing all the good stuff.

'Kids, eh,' said Fi. 'What did Nina say?'

'I imagine you got most of it, but in short – it's a murder. The victim was stabbed in the back, not with anything in the shop or flat. They've taken a scarf and herbs from my stock for comparison and they've dusted for prints. But I can reopen.'

Fi frowned. 'You won't open today, will you? You look exhausted.'

'Thanks. I've had better nights' sleep. Nina seems to think I should open the shop to stop any gossip. If I keep busy, it might stop me dwelling on it.'

'I see what she means,' said Fi, 'but will you be able to cope? You'll be on your own, remember.'

'I'll open when I'm ready, say at half nine or ten, close for lunch, and if I'm flagging in the afternoon I'll shut early. I can always say it's reduced hours because Netta's got the day off.'

'I suppose,' said Fi, though she still looked tired and worried. 'It's just— People can be thoughtless. Someone may upset you without meaning to.'

'I'll be all right,' said Jade, not particularly feeling it. 'I'll refuse to talk about it. I can always ask people to leave.'

'Well, it's up to you,' said Fi. She finished her drink and stood up. 'I'd better get on with sorting the shop out.'

'I'll give you a hand,' said Jade, 'once I've actually made this tea.'

Jade packed away the sofa bed, got changed, and helped Fi move things into position in the main shop. In a quiet moment, she texted Netta to tell her the shop would be open but on reduced hours. The message sent, she scrolled down her contacts until she came to Rick's name. She pressed it, and typed:

Hi, I'm sorry about Tuesday. I was stressed and snapped at you and I shouldn't have. You probably know something happened in the shop yesterday evening. I stayed at Fi's. I'll open later today but Netta won't be in.

After some thought, she added *Sorry again X* and sent the message.

A minute later, her phone rang. *He's losing no time.*

But it was Netta. 'I should have told you before, but I forgot,' she said.

'Hello to you too, Netta,' said Jade. 'Forgot what?'

'A man came in to talk to you the other day, when you were on lunch. He didn't look like one of our customers. I asked if I could help but he said it was you he was after. If he comes in, be careful. I wasn't sure about him at all.'

'What did he look like?'

'He was smart, in a suit, older, shaved head. Not from round here. That's why I thought it was weird.'

'OK, I'll watch out for him. Did he sound angry?'

'No, just as if he really wanted to talk to you.'

'He didn't give a name?'

'I asked, but he said he'd call again and walked out.'

'Odd.' Jade pondered for a moment. 'It's probably nothing, but thanks for letting me know.'

'I thought, what with you reopening... You don't think he did it, did you?'

'I wouldn't worry, Netta,' said Jade. 'You take it easy.'

A message came through from Rick: *I did notice the commotion outside last night. Shall I come over when you're back? Or you could visit me.*

Maybe later, Jade replied, though hanging out with Rick appealed much more than dealing with a bunch of customers who would no doubt pump her for information.

OK, take care X

An hour after opening, Jade wished she had listened to herself. Or, to be more precise, Fi and Rick.

She had arrived at Crystal Dreams to find five or six people waiting, clearly discussing what might have happened the night before. 'I'll be opening at nine thirty,' she said as she unlocked the door, 'and not a moment sooner.'

'What ab—'

Jade cut them off by closing the door.

The shop looked the same as ever. *At least they haven't turned it upside down. Or if they have, they've tidied up.* She wandered around, straightening things, and the scarf display caught her eye. She hurried over, unhooked the ring of white scarves patterned with red skulls and took it to the back room. She would move the others to hide the gap later. Then she went to the herb display and removed the few loose bunches that she kept.

Those things done, Jade went up to her flat for a long shower. Afterwards, she messaged Hugo. For all she knew, Netta had got in first, but hopefully her account of things would be a bit calmer. Then she got ready for the day, choosing a long black skirt and purple top which were, for her, low-key.

By the time she opened the doors, a small crowd had gathered. Jade stood in the doorway and surveyed them. 'I'm guessing you know that the shop was visited by the emergency services last night,' she said. 'I won't be talking about it and I can't answer any questions, so please don't ask me. Thank you.'

Some customers obeyed, but several did not. Jade found herself alternating 'I can't discuss that' with 'No comment'. Most people took it with good grace, but she had to ask a couple of persistent people to leave. *At least takings are up*, she thought, as she put another ten-pound note in the till. *But I'm not sure it's worth it.*

She looked up after deflecting yet another question and saw a small, ratlike man watching her. People had watched her most of the morning, but while everyone else had pretended to be browsing while giving her the side-eye, this chap was openly staring. He was dressed in a silver-grey suit, shiny with wear. Netta's words flashed into Jade's mind: *Be careful.* But this man had a mop of brown hair which stuck out in clumps. Also, he seemed familiar. 'Can I help you?' she asked.

'Came to check on the premises,' he said. 'Seeing as you had the bizzies round last night. I assume they didn't have to break in.'

Of course – her landlord, Mr Snead. Funny that he couldn't be reached about soundproofing or dodgy plumbing, and yet the moment there was a hint of trouble, here he was. 'Everything's fine,' she said.

'It may be fine for you, but it isn't for me. I don't know what's happened, but Magical Moments is closed today and it doesn't take a genius to work out there's a connection.'

'Could you keep your voice down?' Jade muttered. 'The customers will hear you.'

'At least you've got customers,' said Mr Snead. 'If Magical Moments ends up closing, I've got a property vacant. I'm not saying it's your fault exactly—'

'You let another magic shop open in Hazeby?

While I'm right here?'

'Nothing wrong with a bit of competition,' said Mr Snead, grinning. 'A chap's got to make a living.'

'*I've* got to make a living,' said Jade. 'I could do without people making it harder for me. Now, if you'll excuse me.' She turned to the woman waiting patiently at the counter. 'Sorry to keep you.'

'I'm returning this,' said the woman, holding up a book called *Make Your Star Sign Work For You*. 'I've got a gift receipt. Someone bought me it for my birthday. I think she got confused with astronomy.'

'Sure,' said Jade. 'Or you can choose something else from the shop if you prefer.'

'No thanks,' said the woman, looking round with a hint of distaste. 'It's not really my thing.'

Mr Snead chuckled and peeled himself away from the stand he was leaning against. 'Best of British luck to you,' he said, and sauntered off.

Things started to calm down around noon, and by half past twelve there were only two browsers. Jade's stomach made a peculiar noise. Hardly surprising, since she had got through the morning fuelled by strong tea and a battered cereal bar she had found in the counter drawer. *Maybe I could go round to Rick's for lunch. Or if he's busy, I could get a ready meal and eat it in the flat. Lasagne, or a pasta bake…*

Her stodge-themed reverie was interrupted by the shop door opening. Jade straightened up, ready to face yet another curious customer. But the man who came in had no interest in the shelves or displays. He came straight to the counter and smiled at her. He wore a dark-grey suit, well-fitting, with a good-quality white shirt, its top button undone. He looked about her age, but as if he worked out and went on holiday abroad every so often. And his hair was no more than silver fuzz at the sides of his head.

Netta's man, thought Jade. 'Can I help you?' she asked.

'You don't remember me, do you?' The smile broadened. 'Then again, it's been a long, long time. I didn't think I'd ever find you, Ja—' He paused. 'Jade.'

Jade gasped. 'Daz?'

'Yes, though I use Darren now. You're not the only one who's changed a bit.'

Jade stared at him, unable to reply. Images rushed through her head: of throwing up every morning and realising the horrible truth, of Daz promising to look after her, of flinging her belongings in a suitcase, of clearing her bank account and buying a train ticket with the cash so that she couldn't be traced. Of the first time she ran.

CHAPTER 10

Zach was at college, and the Book Barge was busy from the moment the first person entered the shop. Nerys, arriving after the school run, barely had time to take her coat off before she was accosted by two people wanting help because Fi was caught up with three others.

Apart from one message from Jade, saying that she'd opened Crystal Dreams and things were OK so far, Fi heard nothing more from her. No customer mentioned an incident in town, either. Presumably they didn't know, or weren't interested in what might or might not have happened at Crystal Dreams.

Nerys was another matter. It wasn't obvious to begin with. In a rare quiet moment, she showed Fi possible influencers who might publicise the Book Barge, but seemed dubious about whether it would be worth pursuing.

'Zach's more than happy to discuss alternatives,' said Fi. 'He's just trying to think outside the box.'

'What box?'

'Umm… Sometimes, if everyone comes up with mad suggestions, you'll find a solution you never would have got to by being sensible. The principle is that there's no such thing as a bad idea.'

'Yes there is,' Nerys replied. 'Swimming in the Wyvern at this time of year would be a bad idea. Putting my Chester in white clothes then giving him a load of paint would be a bad idea. Doing something dramatic to draw attention to the Book Barge would be a bad idea. *And* sneaky.'

'What do you mean?' said Fi. 'Standing on the deck shouting "Roll up! Roll up! Get your books while they're hot"?'

Nerys looked guilty. 'I mean . . . like get the police round and not say what's happening, to get customers in.'

Fi gave her a hard stare. 'The police wouldn't turn up to help with a publicity stunt. What are you referring to?'

'There was an ambulance then a cop car outside Crystal Dreams last night. Netta Brown didn't go in this morning. And Magical Moments is shut.'

'How did you find that out before coming to work?' Then the penny dropped. 'School-gate gossip? How do the mums and dads and childminders and whatnot know what Netta's doing?'

'Her cousin's little girl's in Chester's class and she – I mean the cousin – is my mate. She messaged Netta to check she was all right after hearing about the ambulance and Netta said she was fine but working from home today. That's odd, isn't it?'

'Not really,' said Fi, hoping her face was as nonchalant as her words. 'Netta does Crystal Dreams's computer work. Some days it's probably easier to crack on at home without interruptions. I'm sure the facts will be out soon, and I'd rather we didn't speculate. People presenting mad ideas as facts isn't fair on anyone, including Netta.'

'I thought you said mad ideas were good.'

'That was in the context of selling books,' said Fi. 'Which is what we should be doing. Go and see what that lady's looking for in the aft section. She's been rummaging for two minutes and your displays are getting in a mess.'

'Aargh! No! I'll sort her out. I mean, help.'

As Nerys rushed to the customer, Fi's phone vibrated the way it did when an email came in.

Dear Ms Booker, Dylan was late for registration this morning, arriving one minute before the register was taken. Please familiarise yourself with the attendance section of the school rules and remind Dylan of them at your earliest convenience. Sixth formers, unless they have express permission to study at home, should adhere to the same hours as lower years. They must arrive in class at least ten minutes prior to registration and stay on the premises until leaving time, except at lunchtime. As this is the first offence, and a number of other pupils were also late today, there will be no sanction. However, should this occur again, Dylan will be subject to an appropriate punishment, which is likely to be a lunchtime or after-school detention.

'So much for school not caring when you turn up,' muttered Fi, wondering why she felt as if there was an underlying threat to put her in detention too. 'Flipping kids.'

She was tempted to ask why arriving with a minute to spare didn't count as 'on time', but that might make things worse for Dylan. Teachers hated argumentative parents. If a number of other pupils had also arrived late, was it because they'd been gossiping about Crystal Dreams? She could only hope that Dylan hadn't mentioned what he knew.

No, she told herself, *he'd have enough sense to keep quiet. Wouldn't he?*

Putting the phone in her pocket, she concentrated on the shop. She'd just have to copy Jade and bury herself in work to try and forget things for a while.

At lunchtime, Fi took Stan for a walk along the towpath. The previous evening, she'd forgotten to respond to Marcus's suggestion of lunch. She was about to message to say that she was free for a short while when she saw him marching towards her.

The usual lurch of excitement she felt was tempered by irritation. Shouldn't he have messaged again when she didn't reply? Or asked how Jade was? Or something?

He kissed her and took her hand. 'I popped by on the off chance you were free. I imagine you were coping with Jade last night and didn't have time to reply.'

'I wasn't coping with her,' said Fi, withdrawing her hand. 'I was comforting her. *You* may be used to handling bodies, but she isn't. She spent ages trying to revive Linzi, not realising she'd been dead for hours.'

'OK. I suppose that was unkind.'

'Yes, it was.'

'You're a good friend to her.'

'I hope so.'

'Come on, Stan's pulling. Where shall we go for lunch? We could grab a sandwich and sit in the park. I don't have time for a pub or café.'

'Nor do I.' Fi let him take her hand again and started towards town. 'I wish you were on the case, and so does Jade, even if you don't appreciate it.'

'She's my friend and you're my girlfriend,' said Marcus. 'It's not appropriate. Surely you both understand that? There's always the risk that I'd be perceived to be prejudiced, and to be honest, I probably would be. Then I might overcompensate and make things worse.'

'I understand that,' said Fi. 'But neither of us were involved. I wasn't even a witness.'

'It would have been better if you hadn't gone there.'

'Jade doesn't have many close friends.'

'She has Rick.'

'They had a row.'

Marcus rolled his eyes. 'Rick Jennings doesn't do rows. It was Jade being defensive or secretive or something, wasn't it?'

'I wasn't there,' snapped Fi. 'How should I know? Jade asked me over to help with Netta. What would you do if a friend asked that of you? Tell them to find someone else?'

They paused on the towpath, Stan whimpering at Fi's ankles. The usual trio of middle-aged male cyclists swerved past, on their way to some hostelry or other. A young couple meandered, cuddled together so closely it was a wonder they could walk at all. They looked as if they were practising for a three-legged race, and if they didn't stop kissing at one-minute intervals there was a risk they'd walk into the river.

'I don't know,' said Marcus. 'I wish you and Jade would stop getting tangled up in suspicious deaths.'

Fi wondered if she should mention what Nina had

told Jade. The fact that she had must be proof positive that Jade wasn't a suspect, since Nina could have concealed the information to see if Jade would let anything slip that incriminated her. 'What can you tell me about the case?' she said. 'Presumably it's discussed between you all.'

'Different teams,' said Marcus. 'We're not supposed to dig or interfere.'

'I don't doubt that,' said Fi. 'But you can't be completely in the dark. Nina knows you know Jade, so she must have asked you something.'

This time it was Marcus who took his hand away. 'Don't you understand this is confidential? It's awkward enough being Jade's friend and knowing you turned up at the premises yesterday evening. Nina's snide little remarks do my head in. There isn't much I can tell you. I gather she's told Jade a few things that, to be honest, I probably wouldn't have. If Jade's not going through one of her secretive phases, I daresay she's told you herself. As I said, I'd rather you weren't involved and I'd rather not discuss it.'

'You're just as secretive.'

'That's unfair.'

Fi looked away, towards Hazeby. Maybe she wasn't being fair, but he wasn't either. Jade could be defensive and secretive. Sometimes it was frustrating, but somehow Fi knew that Jade had been that way for so long that she couldn't help it. She sensed something had happened that, so far, Jade didn't trust Fi enough to explain. It was part of Jade's personality. Fi could cope with it, and Marcus should be able to as well. 'I don't think either of us is being fair.'

'Maybe not. Look…'

He drew Fi onto a muddy piece of grass and lowered his voice, even though no one was in earshot. 'In case she hasn't, what I *do* know and don't mind saying is that Linzi Lawson died from a stab wound. Neither the herbs in her mouth nor the scarf were factors. Someone put her in that bin and when asked, I said it was hard to imagine Jade could do that. The pathologist is yet to provide the autopsy report and the scene of crime team is yet to release its findings. I won't necessarily be party to either. But it's odd about the bolt on the gate.'

'Yes, it is.'

'And it's odd that Jade stores stock in her yard sheds.'

'Is it?'

'Wouldn't it be drier indoors?'

'Doesn't that depend on what she's storing?'

'Perhaps.'

'Are you doing Nina Acaster's job for her?' said Fi.

'Of course I'm not.'

'It seems that way.'

'Does it?' Marcus sighed. 'I can tell you're not in the mood for lunch, and I have to go. Let me know when you want a civilised conversation.'

'That's not—'

Marcus touched her shoulder gently. 'Fair? We're at cross purposes, and maybe we both need to calm down so that we can talk like adults. How about I promise to tell you what I can, if you promise to keep out of it as much as you can?' He kissed her cheek softly, then walked towards town without looking back, hands in pockets and shoulders hunched.

Fi began to go after him, then shook her head. She was sick of being told what to do. And Jade was still on her own in the shop, no doubt overwhelmed with gossip and anxiety.

I'm on my lunch break, she typed. *Shall I bring you a sandwich so you can shut up shop for a bit?*

There was a short burst of three-dot wibbling, then nothing, then:

Not hungry. Talk later.

Fi looked at Stan, who woofed hopefully. 'At least someone wants to have lunch with me,' she said. 'Let's go.' Yet as she made her way to Betsy's, she felt uneasy. She could sort things out with Marcus once they'd both cooled down. But she sensed something was wrong with Jade beyond what had happened the previous evening, and she didn't know how to winkle it out.

CHAPTER 11

Every muscle in Jade's body screamed *Run*, yet she stayed where she was. Despite the instincts of her body, her brain knew there was no point in running. Daz – Darren – looked healthy and fit: the sort of man who hit the gym before work. If she ran, he would catch her easily.

He stood at the counter, smiling, seemingly unaware of the effect he was having on her. Perhaps he was.

'What do you want?' she asked. It was an effort to speak.

'Just to talk,' he said.

'What about?'

He glanced around the shop. The browsers were still browsing. If they had goggled at him, perhaps she'd have had a reason to throw him out. 'I'd rather not have an audience.' Even his voice was different. It was deep, like the voice she remembered, but the vowels had softened and he pronounced the ends of his words.

'What if I don't want to talk to you?' She knew she was being childish: she felt ashamed of herself as the words left her mouth.

'I can't make you. But surely you could spare me a few minutes.'

Damn, he was good. Slick, like his suit.

'Five minutes. No more.' She drew a breath and addressed the room. 'I'm closing for lunch. If you wish to buy something, please bring it to the counter.'

'Thank you,' he said, and stepped aside for the woman bustling towards them, three silver charm necklaces dangling from her fingers.

Jade dealt with her quickly, keeping small talk to the minimum, and a few minutes later she shut the door behind her departing customers and turned the sign round.

I should take him into the back room, she thought. *I should offer him tea.* Instead, she returned to the counter. 'Go on, then,' she said. 'Talk.'

'Your shop looks great,' he said. 'It must have taken a lot of work.'

'It did.' She eyed him. 'I'm guessing that's not why you're here.'

'It's been a long time, hasn't it?' He thought for a moment. 'Twenty-six years?'

'More or less.'

For a moment, Jade remembered herself as a schoolgirl in a science lesson, learning about magnets. 'You know the north pole of a magnet is attracted to the south pole of another,' the teacher said. 'Now try and bring two north poles together.' She recalled how the magnets had repelled each other. They were weak, so it was possible to force them to touch, but they jumped apart the moment they were released. That was how this felt: trying to reconcile this sharp-suited, quietly spoken man with noisy, shiftless Daz. She could see a resemblance at the core: the brown eyes still had a deep furrow between the eyebrows. In the old days, Daz had frowned at the injustice when protesting to teachers that it wasn't his fault and someone must have planted the ciggies on him, or that he had definitely handed in his homework but the teacher must have lost it. It never worked. Jade wondered if Darren ever made excuses, and suspected he did not.

She hadn't gone out with him at school. That had come later, when she'd gone to the pub after a hard shift and found him there. ''Ello,' he had said, sliding onto the barstool next to her. 'Wanna drink?'

Her mother disapproved of Daz. Jade didn't approve of him herself, particularly, but he was someone to hang out with. A reason not to go straight home from work and stay there, watching TV with her mum.

'He doesn't even have a job,' her mother grumbled. 'Is he looking?'

'He's between jobs at the moment,' said Jade.

What that meant, in practice, was that Daz favoured jobs which were cash in hand. On-the-quiet jobs, on-the-side jobs. He also bought things cheap and sold them on, sometimes in the pub. Jade didn't care to ask where the things came from. If she had, Daz would probably have tapped the side of his nose and made some remark along the lines of 'Ask me no questions and I'll tell you no lies'. She wasn't bothered, since she and Daz weren't serious. She had no intention of getting serious with Daz.

The man in front of her coughed, an excuse-me kind of cough, and Jade came to with a start. 'So what do you do now?' she asked. 'Still wheeler-dealing?'

He grinned. 'In a way.' Jade tried to imagine him in a flat cap at a market stall, but it didn't fit at all. 'I work in tech.'

Jade almost said *Like Hugo*, but stopped herself in time. 'How did that happen?' she asked, instead.

'When you got pregnant, I knew I had to make something of myself instead of bumming around. So I found a training scheme and got on it. That was easy, because they were desperate to get me off benefits. And I liked it. I was hoping you'd come back and see that I'd changed.' He looked as if he wanted to say more, but didn't.

'How did you find me?' Jade asked, to break the silence. The longer it continued, the guiltier she felt.

'I didn't set out to find you,' said Darren. 'I figured that if you didn't want to be found, it wasn't fair of me to search for you. It happened by chance. Recently, I wrote an article for a small publication – a newsletter-type thing – about the role of technology in business. I did it as a favour to a mate. Anyway, he sent me a copy of the newsletter and there you were on the cover. I wavered when I saw the name in the caption, but I was convinced it was you, so I decided to see if I was right.'

'*BizTech Retail News*?'

'That's it. The piece I wrote is on page two.'

I knew I should have refused to be in that photograph, thought Jade. *I only did it because Netta wanted me to. Now look what's happened.* She opened the counter drawer, pulled out the newsletter and turned to the second page. The headline was *The Frictionless Transaction*, and underneath it said: *Integration expert Darren Hartley sings the praises of automation for businesses of all sizes.* Her eyes must have skimmed that more than once, never expecting to find Daz there. *Netta would read that. Hugo probably would, too.*

'Can I ask you something?' said Darren.

Jade was tempted to say no, but it didn't feel fair.

He had answered her questions. 'Yeah,' she said.

'Why did you run away?' His brown eyes were very steady in their gaze. He had stopped smiling. He didn't look angry, but he did look hurt. 'I said I'd take care of you when you told me. I said you could stay home with the baby or return to work, whatever you wanted.'

Jade shrugged to give herself time. 'I had reasons,' she said, eventually.

He took a step back. 'Sorry, I know that must be a difficult question.' He paused. 'Your mum told me you had a baby boy.'

'Yes.' Jade hadn't considered that Daz might have talked to her mum, since they'd never been on good terms. Her disappearing act had probably brought them together. She winced at the thought of them discussing her. All her mum had ever said on the phone was that Daz had asked after her, to which Jade either replied 'Huh,' or 'I hope you didn't tell him anything.'

'Would you mind if I contacted him?'

Yes, I would. The pair of you talking about me, the stupid decisions I've made and the things I've run away from more times than I can count. But she saw the yearning behind his carefully neutral expression. So all she said was 'I don't suppose I can stop you.'

'Thanks.' A friendly smile. 'I've—'

'Look, I've got things to do,' said Jade. 'Errands to

run.'

'OK.' He reached into the breast pocket of his nice suit and put a business card on the counter. A good-quality card, in colour. *Darren Hartley, Head of Integration, InfoWorks*, with an email address and phone number. 'In case you want to get in touch with me,' he said. 'I hope you don't mind that I came to look you up. It's been nice to see you again. Maybe we can talk when it's – less of a bolt from the blue.'

'Maybe,' said Jade. 'Anyway.' She walked to the door and opened it.

Darren followed her and paused on the threshold. 'I'm glad you're doing OK.' She couldn't meet his eyes. 'I worried about you.' His smile was more sad than happy now. He walked out of Crystal Dreams and down the street.

Jade closed the door, put the catch on and made sure the sign still said *Closed*. But she didn't busy herself with errands as she had told Darren she would. She went into the back room, sat at the little table and stared into space, too stunned to think straight. Occasionally, a thought raced through her brain – *What will Hugo say? Will he still speak to me?* – but mostly the inside of her head felt like a bleak void, filled only with the howling of a cold, cold wind.

CHAPTER 12

Jade made no response when Fi messaged to say she was always there if needed. Fi decided Jade had probably been busy, and maybe wanted a lunch break without talking.

It'll be good for her, Fi told herself, as she dealt with her own exhausting afternoon. *It'll take her mind off things. But I'm sure she's worrying about something else. Rick? Hugo? She can't have been arrested. Nerys would have heard on the grapevine, I'm sure, and Marcus would tell me… Wouldn't he?*

Nerys left for the school run shortly before three and Dylan ambled in at four, half an hour after he was supposed to be home. Fi was too busy to do anything but give him a hard stare. It did the trick. He dropped coat and bag behind the counter and tackled the queue of people waiting to pay while Fi helped a customer trace an out-of-print philosophy book.

'I can't recall the exact title, but it has to do with birds,' he said. 'The author's first name is Jules. Victorian, maybe. But the cover's definitely blue with silver smoke. Or perhaps it was red with gold frogs…'

Fi turned the computer to show him an image of a blue book decorated with golden reeds, lily pads and swooping swallows. '*The Bird* by Jules Michelet?'

'You're a marvel.'

'With that cover, it'll be over a hundred pounds. There are cheaper later editions for less than twenty.'

'That's the one I want, m'dear. Don't forget your commission. Now, what do I do?'

When the shop was empty and they could close up, Dylan disappeared into the galley. Fi felt herself boil up with a combination of disappointment and irritation. She messaged Jade again. No response. She dialled Jade's number, but it rang until voicemail kicked in.

Then Dylan reappeared with two mugs of coffee and some stale biscuits on a plate. 'Sit down, Mum. You look like you've had enough. I'll finish up in here, then we can watch early-evening rubbish on TV.'

She raised her eyebrows.

'Um, maybe don't eat a biscuit,' he said. 'Think of it as a virtual snack, not a real one. I found them at the back of the cupboard. It's the thought that counts.' He gave her a lopsided, pleading grin, just as he used to do as a child. She sensed he was trying to make peace and returned the smile to encourage him.

'There's a new packet of Hobnobs. I'll get them.'

'Hidden? Sneaky.'

'If you knew where I kept them you'd scoff a packet a day. I can't afford it.'

'Rude.'

'But fair.'

Fi retrieved the Hobnobs from a box that had once held spirulina, a health food even she wouldn't eat again and somewhere Dylan would never investigate, then sat down with him on the sofa and waited.

He picked up the remote control but didn't switch the TV on. Without looking at her, he said, 'I nearly got a detention today because I was "late" for school.' He made speech marks in the air and rolled his eyes. 'If you didn't know, now you do. If you did, thanks for not having a go at me. And if school had a go at you, I'm sorry. It's ridiculous, though. I'm not a year seven. I'm old enough to . . . to smoke and buy a lottery ticket, and I'll be old enough to drive in a few months, but they're still treating me like I'm eleven. I wish I'd gone to college.'

'They didn't do the right courses.'

'Yeah, but...' Dylan tapped the remote-control buttons. 'How's Jade?'

Fi sipped her coffee, wondering how to answer. She checked her phone but there were still no messages. 'Pretty stressed. Who wouldn't be?'

'People are saying stuff.'

'What people?'

'Kids.'

'What stuff?'

Dylan shrugged. 'That's why I'm late home. I was arguing. Most kids are for her. Crystal Dreams is popular, like I told her. But everyone knows something happened there last night and someone was taken away as if they were dead. It's all a bit... Someone said "Is it a publicity stunt cos Halloween's coming up?" I didn't know what to say. I mean, given what Jade said this morning—'

'Oh Dylan, you didn't repeat it?'

'Of course I didn't! What do you take me for?' He scowled.

'Sorry.'

'Hmm. Anyway, I said that Jade wouldn't do stunts. Whatever's going on will be investigated properly, and then we'll know.' He wrinkled his nose and stared at the remote control. 'Then...'

'Then what?'

'Then someone said "You would say that. Your mum's best mates with Jade *and* she's . . . going out with the police. Don't tell Booker anything cos he'll snitch," and they all laughed.'

I bet it was coarser than that, thought Fi, feeling herself blush. 'All of them?'

'No, just the in-crowd. But—'

'Try not to let them get to you,' said Fi. 'If it keeps up...'

Dylan cleared his throat and turned on the TV. 'Enough soppy stuff. Pass us the biscuits. At least Marcus isn't in charge. That makes life easier, doesn't it?'

As if on cue, a message from Marcus came through.

I'm sorry about earlier. Maybe I didn't explain myself very well. I really am tied up in this other case and have to go to London tonight. Any chance of kissing and making up before I do? If not . . . maybe when I'm back you'll have stopped wanting to kill me.

Fi felt a mixture of emotions. She didn't want Marcus to go anywhere. She wanted him to stay and investigate Linzi's death. But if he had to go, she didn't want him to leave without making peace first.

OK, she replied. *When and where?*

I'm standing on the towpath right now if that helps.

'Find some rubbish to watch, Dylan,' she said. 'I'm going out for fresh air.'

Marcus was outside, hunched in his coat. They stood for a moment, looking at each other, then Fi stepped into his arms.

'I'm sorry,' they said, simultaneously.

'I'm worried about Jade,' said Fi. 'I don't think she's handling this well, but I swear she has nothing to do with what happened.'

'I believe you,' said Marcus. 'I'm sorry I made her sound like a drama queen. I totally understand why she called you and why you went. Nina, much as she irritates me, is a good cop. She'll investigate thoroughly and fairly. All I can do is be a character witness. I said I thought that if Jade felt threatened by a business rival she'd leave town, not attack. Something in her personality makes her inclined to run. Do you agree?'

'Yes. I wish I knew what.'

'Maybe you'll never know.' Marcus hugged her tighter. 'Maybe Jade just needs a friend to stop her running. I have to leave for London, and that means I may not hear much about the Linzi Lawson case unless Nina tells me. But I promise to tell you anything you should know, and do anything I can to help. Do you believe that?'

'Yes. And I promise not to dig where I shouldn't.'

'Thanks. Now then, where's that kiss?'

All too soon, he was striding towards the station, leaving Fi on the towpath. She couldn't tell him that she wasn't particularly reassured or that she felt guilty about making a promise not to dig. 'Where I shouldn't' was very different to 'where *you* think I shouldn't'. She hoped she wouldn't have to dig and that, against all the odds, he'd come back from London and take over from Nina.

Poor Jade. Alone in the shop, worrying herself

sick. Fi could only hope she wasn't planning to run away, as she always had before.

Maybe Jade just needs a friend to stop her running.

Fi stood on the deck and rang Jade's number. There was no reply. She sent a message, then a text. Neither showed as read. *Where is she?*

Then Fi went cold. *What if Linzi wasn't a victim because of who she was, but what she was? Some people complained about the occult when Jade opened Crystal Dreams: they didn't grasp what she was actually doing. What if they've applied the same logic to Magical Moments? What if they're targeting people with those kinds of shops? Maybe Jade's at risk. Maybe, when she didn't want me round at lunchtime, she was under threat and I didn't realise.*

Fi couldn't shake off the feeling that something was wrong. She ran into the boat and grabbed her handbag. 'We don't have anything in for dinner,' she said to Dylan. 'Fancy a homemade curry?'

'Extra hot?' said Dylan. 'Poppadums and fancy naan bread and onion bhajis?'

'Yes. I might be a while.'

'Want help?'

'No, just get on with any homework you don't have. I'll be back as soon as I can.'

Fi hurried to Crystal Dreams. The closed sign was up, which was no surprise, but it wasn't entirely dark.

As all the internal doors were open, she could see as far as the yard, where coloured fairy lights twinkled. She could go round the back, but if the gate to the alley was bolted it wouldn't help. Jade must be inside somewhere.

Fi hammered on the door.

A couple walking along the pavement paused. 'She's shut, love,' said the woman, pointing at the sign.

'You the police?' said the man. 'Undercover? Police were here last night.'

'She's my friend,' said Fi. 'It's a personal visit.'

'Oh, right. Maybe she forgot you were coming.' The woman shrugged and they carried on walking.

Fi hammered again.

Finally, she saw Jade advance and peer through the glass. 'Let me in!' Fi mouthed.

Jade hesitated, unlocked the door, let Fi in, relocked it and walked towards the back room without saying a word.

Fi followed her in confusion. There was no sign of violence or forced entry. All the theories she'd thought up dissolved. She'd been ridiculous. Her fear and anxiety, the exhausting day on the Book Barge, the snarky email from school, Dylan's bullies, the row with Marcus and knowing he was going away – everything bubbled up and burst out before she could stop herself.

'Is that it?' she snapped. 'No "Thanks for ringing me, messaging me, worrying about me, asking Marcus to help, then coming round to make sure I'm not dead"? Clearly not.'

Jade turned. 'What?' Her face was stricken. She looked beyond running, as if all the fight had drained out of her. So much for being a friend.

'I'm sorry,' said Fi, her anger dissipating. 'I'm so sorry. I didn't mean any of that. I was so worried about you, and when I didn't hear…'

To her horror, Jade crumpled into a chair and sobbed. No snapping back, no anger, no sarcasm. She cried like a child, tears pouring down her face without hindrance, without words.

Fi dropped to her side and pulled Jade into her arms. 'I'm so sorry,' she said. 'What's wrong? What's really wrong? I know it's not just Linzi. Don't you trust me enough by now to tell me what it is?'

CHAPTER 13

'I don't trust people, you know that,' Jade got out between sobs. 'I don't even trust myself. As for him... Maybe I should – I should have listened, but I didn't, and now look.' All the things she had done wrong in her life crowded in on her, and she put her face in her hands.

'Shh,' said Fi, rubbing her back. It was comforting, but Jade also felt rather as if she were a baby being burped. 'You don't have to talk. I'm really sorry.'

'So am I,' murmured Jade. Gradually, her urge to sob subsided. She wondered how many people Fi had comforted in her life who also didn't deserve it. 'You're a good friend.'

'So are you, when you reply to messages.' Fi caught her eye and Jade managed a tiny smile. 'Tea?'

'I can make it.'

'I know you can, but you need looking after.' Fi

got up and filled the kettle. 'I'm just glad you're safe. I thought the murderer might have got to you too.'

'Murderer? He isn't—'

'Who isn't?' Fi was standing with her back to Jade, getting mugs out of the cupboard.

'No one.' Jade wiped her eyes on her sleeve. Her face was sticky with tears.

'I assume you don't mean Rick,' said Fi, finding a space for the mugs among the stacks of subscription boxes, then putting teabags in them.

'Course not. Forget I said it.'

Fi turned round and leaned against the worktop. 'Jade, you're upset over something and I want to help. Please will you talk to me? If this "him" you're talking about isn't Rick, then who is it?'

Jade considered what to say. She could refuse to answer, of course, but that felt wrong after the fright she'd given Fi. 'Someone I used to know a long time ago,' she said. 'He came to the shop earlier.'

'Oh.' Fi's brow furrowed slightly. Jade could imagine what was going on in her head. Considering the options, what was likely and what was not. 'Did you argue?'

Jade shook her head.

'He didn't—' Fi crouched next to her and took her hand. 'He didn't threaten you, did he? Or hurt you?'

'Nothing like that,' Jade muttered. 'Look, I really don't want to talk about it. I know you want to help, but I'd rather forget it happened.'

'OK.' Fi straightened up and leaned on the worktop with her back to Jade, waiting for the kettle.

Have I offended her? thought Jade. 'It isn't you,' she said, 'it's me.'

'You sound like one of my ex-boyfriends,' said Fi, not looking round. 'When they broke up with me, it was never my fault.'

'Whereas it's always mine.'

'Don't be silly.'

'I'm not being. Whenever things go wrong, it's almost always because of something stupid I've done.'

'Oh, Jade.' The kettle pinged and Fi drowned the teabags in boiling water. 'Why are you so down on yourself? You've built a successful business and Hugo's a great kid. Young man, I mean.'

'No thanks to me, and if I'd made better decisions…'

'Like what?' Fi poured milk in the mugs and gave the teabags a thorough squidge before binning them. 'Can you hold this without spilling it over yourself?'

'I expect so.' Jade took the mug and held it for a few moments, then risked a sip. 'Thanks. What a mess.'

'I take it you don't mean the room,' said Fi, sitting in the other chair and sipping her own drink. 'Anyway, you'll feel better once you've got all these boxes collected. Why don't you make that your first job next time you open?'

'Uh huh.' Jade sipped again and closed her eyes. Even the thought of arranging a parcel collection felt overwhelming. *I don't want Jim coming here to collect the boxes and looking at me as if I've killed someone. I have to get away from this: people judging me and talking about me. I want to go to a place where people don't know me.* She wondered how long was left on the shop lease. Mr Snead would never let her go early, not with the threat of Magical Moments quitting. *I could just go. Pack Bertha, drive off in the night and leave this mess behind.*

Then she imagined Hugo saying 'Not again, Mummy.' Rick's face when he came round and discovered she had gone. Netta, coming to work and finding there was no business to promote and plan for any more. And of course, Fi.

She opened her eyes. Fi was gazing at her. The little furrow between her eyebrows, which showed when she was pondering or worried, had deepened. 'Are you planning to run away?' she asked, softly.

'I'd like to,' said Jade. 'I was thinking about it. But I can't, can I? There's subscription boxes to get out and Netta to keep in check.'

'And tea to drink. Though yours is in imminent danger of going in your lap.'

'Sorry.' Jade took a swig.

'You don't have to apologise to me,' said Fi. 'It's

your lap that's in danger. Although the tea's probably cooled down enough to be unpleasant rather than dangerous.'

'True.'

They sat in companionable silence, drinking their tea. Jade wasn't sure how Fi had managed it, but her brain felt less as if it would burst. 'Thanks,' she said.

'I know you don't want to discuss whatever it is, and I can't help with that. But maybe we can do something about this murder.' Fi's mouth pursed as if she had eaten a slice of lemon. 'I'm not sure how, mind you. I just saw Marcus. If anything, he's more private than Nina. He warned me off.'

Jade snorted. 'Did he, now.'

'He tried. I said I wouldn't poke my nose anywhere I shouldn't. However, my opinion on what I should and shouldn't do isn't necessarily the same as Marcus's.'

Jade frowned. 'Don't do anything you're uncomfortable with, Fi. Marcus is trying to keep you out of danger. He's a good man and he cares about you.' All at once, Daz – Darren – came into her head. After she had run away and effectively dumped him, he had turned his life around, respected her privacy and asked nothing of her. She bit her lip.

'I'm not sure I approve of this new, cautious Jade,' said Fi, with a half smile. 'How will I get into scrapes if you make me wrap up warm and take a flask and a packet of sandwiches?'

'Well, if anyone's getting into scrapes, it's you,' Jade replied. 'I can't start interrogating people or sneaking around. That would bring Nina round here faster than you can say "obstructing a police officer". She's probably on the watch for you too, seeing as firstly, she knows you're my friend, and secondly, we've both got a history of this sort of thing.'

'She can't stop me living my life,' said Fi. 'If I want to go shopping in your rival establishment, there's no law against it. Same as there's no law against me browsing the internet.'

'If you do, use an incognito browser at least. You should probably speak to Hugo before you go anywhere near a screen.'

'How is Hugo?' Fi asked, casually.

I wish I knew, thought Jade. *If Darren's got in touch...* She shivered. 'Fine, the last time we spoke,' she said, trying to match Fi's casual tone. 'He's worried about the murder, but I reassured him.'

Fi put a hand on her arm. 'I wish you'd tell me what it is. Surely it can't be that bad.'

Jade shook her head.

'OK. But I need my investigation buddy back.'

'I wish I could get involved,' said Jade. 'We're still partners, right? Fitch and Booker, private eyes.'

'Alphabetical order, if you please,' said Fi. 'Booker and Fitch.'

'Our partnership isn't a bookshop or a library,' said Jade. 'But yeah, OK. For this case, at least. As I'm hamstrung by circumstance.'

'You are, rather,' said Fi. 'The quicker we find out who did it and get them arrested, the quicker things will return to normal.'

'Mmm.' Jade didn't feel as if anything would ever be normal again. It was as if someone had taken the nice contained bubble she had created for herself and shaken it violently. Everything was raining down on her faster than she could cope with.

Fi smiled. 'Normal for you, then.'

'Touché.' But in spite of herself, Jade felt less like digging a big hole, getting in and pulling it in after her, or going to bed and staying there for the rest of the year. She looked at the table, still piled high with subscription boxes. 'I'll get those shifted ASAP.'

'Good idea,' said Fi. 'Make room for your investigation notebook. Now, do you want to go shopping with me, then come to mine for a proper hot curry?'

'I'd love to.' Jade smiled, willing the lump in her throat to go away. 'I'll get the wine.'

I don't deserve Fi, she thought. *I know I don't. But I'm so glad that she sees something in me, and I won't let her down.* She locked up the shop, and they walked along the street together.

CHAPTER 19

If Dylan was surprised when Fi told him to go out with his friends on a school night, he wasn't daft enough to say so. He shovelled in his curry and grabbed the spare onion bhajis to take to Alfie's before Fi could argue.

'When do you next need to be at the theatre for rehearsals?' she called, as he snatched up his backpack.

'Saturday morning, but I was—'

'But nothing,' said Fi. 'They're paying you, and it'll go towards your A level and your future career.'

'The gig's on Saturday evening! I'll be shattered if I'm working in the morning and gigging in the evening. That's important to my career, too.'

'So have a lie in on Sunday. I won't stop you.'

'Huh.' Dylan gave Jade a swift hug. 'Don't let things get you down,' he said. 'And don't let Mum boss you about.' Then he dashed from the boat.

'Boss me about as much as you like,' said Jade, gloomily. 'It saves thinking.'

'Your obedience level is probably the same as Dylan's.'

'He's a good kid,' said Jade. 'But then, you're a normal family.'

'Hugo's a good kid too, and my family's the same as yours. We both brought up our sons alone.'

'I meant your wider family. And Dylan had *you* bringing him up. Hugo had me. I don't know how he turned out so well.' Jade sounded on the verge of tears.

'Because you love him,' said Fi. 'You're a good mother. Now, let's stop talking about things that don't matter and concentrate on what does. I'll get my laptop. What should we search for? I take it you haven't done any research yourself.'

Jade waggled her hand. 'I did a bit when Magical Moments arrived in town. After I found Linzi in the b-bin, there was no way I'd look again. Nina might put two and two together and make forty-two.'

'If you'd murdered anyone you'd look them up beforehand, not afterwards,' said Fi.

'Which is what I did. But it was top-level business stuff. Nothing personal.'

'Did you use an incognito browser?'

'That makes me think of a shadowy customer with

a fedora pulled over their eyes,' said Jade, with a tiny spark of a smile.

'Does Hugo know about the murder?'

'Yes, but he doesn't know how I felt when Magical Moments opened, or that I argued with Linzi in the shop, or about Sneaky Snead's hints. Netta told him I was upset, but when he offered to come down I said no. He probably only wants to see Netta, anyway.'

'He'll want to see both of you.' Fi filled the dishwasher, then plonked her laptop on the table and opened it. 'Does he know about your visitor today? The person from a long time ago?'

'It's nothing to do with him.' Jade sat hunched, hands clasped. There was something very vulnerable about her: her eyes flickered under her lids as she chased thoughts. Who was the man who'd unnerved her so much? Was he hounding Jade over her choice of business? Were her earlier suspicions correct? Was Jade in danger?

'I know you'd rather not talk about him,' Fi said. 'But is he opposed to Crystal Dreams in principle?'

Jade looked up, startled. 'What?'

'Magic. Witches. Spells.'

'I doubt it. His opinion's irrelevant, anyway.' Jade pulled her chair forward. 'Let's get on, shall we?'

'All right,' said Fi, giving up. Hopefully it would come out eventually. 'Let's go.'

Where to begin, she thought. A general search for

Linzi would no doubt bring up newspaper reports on the murder. That would be starting in the wrong place, especially as the police hadn't revealed a great deal.

Social media should provide background information, whether it was genuine or tweaked for public consumption. No one was ever really themselves on social media, but you could read between the lines. However, Fi couldn't see how to interrogate social media without logging into one of her own accounts. The only option was to create a fake one, which would take ages, partly because it would involve buying a pay-as-you-go mobile first.

Her phone buzzed.

Safely in London. It'll be an early night tonight. Got to prove to the Met that provincial cops can do more than herd sheep and arrest people for cycling in the dark without lights tomorrow. Love you x

She tapped a reply. *I'll ring you at ten. Love you too x*

'Dylan?' said Jade.

'Marcus.'

'Is he still telling you to keep your nose out?'

'No,' said Fi. 'You know what? I'm going to risk it. Forget the incognito browser. And it'll look more sneaky if Nina finds out I created fake accounts. I'll fish under my own name. As I said, hundreds of people will look, so the chance of me being spotted is pretty low.'

She topped up their glasses and opened every social media app she had. 'Whatever did we do before these were invented?' she said, rolling her eyes. 'It's ridiculous, I can't keep up. Ugh, more influencers. I'm not sure if Zach's a genius or mad.'

'What?'

'Never mind. What next?'

'I found Linzi on the Magical Moments accounts and on her own,' said Jade, pulling her chair closer. 'I'm sure she's on that professional one as an individual. Hugo keeps telling me to join it. LinkyMacLinkface.'

'I know the one you mean: I'm a member. I should be able to find her. Unless someone's closed it and all her other personal accounts.'

'It's too soon,' said Jade. 'It's not the first thing you think of when someone's died, is it? I don't even know how you would do it. Isn't it supposed to be quite difficult?'

'Good point.' Fi searched for Linzi's personal accounts. Most were restricted to friends – but some weren't. Either way, there were plenty of photographs of Linzi in business wear, looking every inch the manager, and others of awards and trophies and statements charting her progress up the corporate ladder. There were only a few photographs of groups, mostly of Linzi with her staff in front of a Magical

Moments display.

Stan came out of his basket, stretched, jumped in Jade's lap and curled up. She scratched his ears absently.

Fi opened up the Magical Moments accounts next. On each was a pinned post with a headshot of Linzi, glowing praise and a brief message mourning her passing.

'Hmm,' she said. 'There are lots of likes, but comments are turned off. Odd.'

'Yes, it is,' said Jade. 'You'd think they'd let her colleagues express their condolences.'

'Mmm.' Searching was making Fi's head and eyes hurt. 'Let's check LinkyMacLinkface. It might show when she started working for Magical Moments.'

There was another headshot of Linzi looking professional: smart, chin up, her smile proud and polite. If she hadn't known otherwise and someone had said Linzi was the CEO of Magical Moments, Fi would have taken their word for it. Maybe that was where she'd expected to end up. According to her CV, Linzi's race up the promotion ladder had been rapid. She'd been responsible for stores in big towns and cities, the latest being the Manchester branch, a flagship store.

Fi sat back. 'I love Hazeby,' she said, 'but it's not a logical place to go after Manchester. I'd expect London next, wouldn't you?'

'Perhaps she blotted her copybook.'

'I don't get that impression from the company's praise.'

'You're not supposed to speak ill of the dead,' said Jade.

'Yeah, but there are ways of saying things that mean everyone knows the person wasn't a great worker. Those seemed genuine, if impersonal.'

'I've never worked for a big corporation,' said Jade. 'How well do the people at the top know the people further down the ladder?'

Fi shuddered. 'Don't remind me how soulless it can be. And yes, you've got a point. When someone retired, died, or moved on, the people at the top got a colleague to write something then turned it into corporate speak. Maybe that's why the statement about Linzi is so clinical. But why did she come to Hazeby? I can't see a high-flyer going from Manchester to a small country town.'

'You did.'

'Not while I was flying. I moved when I decided I wanted a different life. Does it mean Linzi wanted a slower pace, too? Or did the company promote someone over her and put her out to grass, even though she seemed successful?'

'You mean, did she jump or was she pushed?'

'How can we find out?' Fi toggled between the various tabs on the laptop but nothing struck her. She took a sip of wine and contemplated Jade. 'Or – I have to suggest this – was she running from something? Something, or someone, that followed her here?'

Jade stared into her own wine, scratched Stan's ears, then looked up. 'Maybe. I'd have thought I'd recognise it in someone else, but if they were after my business...' She cleared her throat. 'OK, so that's socials, as Netta would say. What else?'

'Just the newspaper articles, I guess,' said Fi, opening a new tab and making a search. There were so many that she was surprised neither her mother or mother-in-law had rung to complain about another murder.

Each article reproduced the statement from Magical Moments they had seen on social media. But the reporters had also interviewed Linzi's colleagues.

'We'll miss her so much,' said assistant manager Harvey Batchelor. 'It's such a shame. Her husband must be beside himself. I don't know how we'll cope when we reopen on Friday.'

Shop assistant Charlie Furniss told us, 'She'll be missed. Magical Moments was her whole life.'

Ms Lawson's husband, Joe, has so far been too distraught to talk to reporters.

There was no mention of children.

'I can't think of anything else we can find online,' said Fi. 'Can you?'

Jade shook her head. 'We'll have to sleep on it. I'd better go home.'

'You're welcome to stay.'

'Nah. I'd better face the flat and you probably want to call Marcus and whisper sweet nothings. I suppose I should call Hugo and tell him . . . something.' She looked pensive.

'I'll walk you back.'

'Don't be silly.'

'Stan needs a walk,' said Fi. 'In fact, I'll leave him with you. He'll like that and he'll be company for you overnight.'

Jade glanced at Stan, who said 'Rrrerrfff' and wagged his tail. 'How will I get him back to you? I'll probably be opening up on my own again tomorrow morning.'

'I'll fetch him when I visit Magical Moments,' said Fi, closing down the laptop.

'You what?'

'It's the only thing left,' said Fi. 'And of the two of us, I'm the one who can do it.'

CHAPTER 15

Jade woke feeling comparatively rested the next morning. She reached for her phone: the display said *7.50*. 'That's very civilised,' she murmured. For a moment she lay in bed, thinking of nothing and enjoying it. Then she stretched. *I should probably get up. There's something I was going to do—*

'Rrrerrfff?'

Jade almost jumped out of bed. 'What the— Stan!'

'Rrrerrfff!' Stan ran to her and put his front paws on the bed, tail wagging furiously.

'Good morning to you too.' But even Stan's enthusiastic greeting couldn't counteract the chilling effect his presence had on Jade. Everything came flooding back – the murder, falling out with Fi, however briefly, and Daz turning up like a bolt from the blue. She winced, and she could have sworn that remembering yesterday's events had actually brought on a headache. 'Tea,' she said firmly, 'and breakfast. Yes, for you as well.'

Stan had a lovely time investigating every corner of Jade's flat while she made herself tea and toast and put dog biscuits in a bowl for him. 'You're inquisitive, aren't you?' she observed. 'I wish we could use you on the case somehow.'

'Rrrerrfff.' Stan's tail moved more tentatively.

'You are a *very* good boy.'

'Rrrerrfff!' Stan's tail thumped against the cupboard where Jade kept her pans.

Now that she had remembered the full situation, Jade decided to leave opening until nine thirty. If she was single-handed again, she would need to conserve her energy. However, as she was listening to the eight-thirty news on the radio, she heard a familiar click and creak downstairs. *Netta*.

'Good grief,' she muttered. 'Stan, stay there a minute, will you.'

Stan woofed softly and dropped to the carpet, his eyes on her the whole time.

'You're fab,' Jade told him. She retied her dressing gown, checked her front for toast crumbs or jam stains and went down.

Netta was staring into the open till. Then she looked at Jade. 'You didn't cash up last night,' she said.

'No. Stuff on my mind. It's a long story.'

'Oh, OK.'

'And I haven't got the subscription boxes collected yet. But I will today.'

'Good,' Netta said, gazing around her as if the shop had transformed overnight.

'Netta, are you sure you should be in? You don't seem quite yourself.'

'I'm fine,' said Netta. 'I'm sorry about yesterday. I just—'

'You don't have to explain,' said Jade. 'It was awful, and you were right to stay home. I kind of wish I hadn't opened yesterday, either.'

Netta stared at her. 'Why? Did something happen?'

It certainly did, thought Jade, *but not in the way you mean.* 'Nothing too terrible,' she said. 'People being nosy. The usual.'

'Oh.' Netta closed the till, which pinged. She took in Jade's pyjamas and dressing gown. 'I was… I assumed we'd be opening at nine as usual.'

'To be honest, I was going to leave it until half past. But now you're here, I'll get ready.' She turned to go upstairs, then remembered her house guest. 'By the way, Stan stayed over last night.'

Netta's expression was a mixture of confusion and embarrassment. 'Not – I thought you were—'

'Fi's dog,' said Jade. 'I haven't taken to bringing strange men home.'

'Oh!' Netta giggled. Then she looked worried.

'You won't bring him in the shop, will you? I'm not keen on dogs. Plus it's the wrong vibe.'

'He's ever so good,' said Jade. 'Sits on command and everything. I don't want to leave him upstairs on his own.'

'I'm a bit allergic to pet hair,' said Netta, nervously.

'How about he stays in the back room?' said Jade. 'Fi's picking him up later, anyway.'

Netta considered. 'OK,' she said, eventually. 'As long as I don't have to – take him out or anything.'

'That's a point,' said Jade. 'I'll do that as soon as I'm ready. You can open up, can't you?'

Netta laughed. 'Of course I can! I open up more than you do.'

'OK, OK.' Jade stepped back, hands raised. 'I'll take care of the savage beast, and you can look after the customers.'

Jade took Stan for a little walk, since she felt rather guilty for confining him to the back room. 'It's not my fault,' she told him. 'It's my finicky assistant.'

'Rrrerrfff,' said Stan, and watered the lamp post.

When Jade returned at ten past nine, the shop was distinctly busy. 'We wondered where you were,' said a woman who she dimly remembered was a good customer for silver charms and rabbit's feet. 'I was a bit worried, frankly.'

'Dog-walking duty,' said Jade, indicating Stan,

who wagged his tail.

'A dog?' She sounded affronted. 'You can't have a dog! A cat, or maybe an owl…'

'I can have whatever pets I like,' said Jade. 'In any case, this isn't my dog. I'm dog-sitting for a friend.'

'That's the dog from the Book Barge,' said a man in red trousers who she didn't remember seeing in the shop before. He crouched. 'You're Stan, aren't you?'

'Rrrerrfff!' Stan thumped his tail.

Jade glanced at Netta, who was rather pale. 'I'll take him in the back,' she said. 'Come on, Stan, let's get you settled.'

She brought Stan's food and water bowls and put his bed in the corner by the door to the yard. 'Sorry you're in chokey,' she told him. 'Hopefully Fi will fetch you soon. On her way to doing some investigating.'

Stan went to his bed and lay down, still looking expectant.

'I can't magic her here,' Jade reasoned. 'Anyway, I'd better go and help in the shop.'

However, when she went through, there was little to do. While there were plenty of people in the shop, they seemed more interested in chatting than buying. *Hmm*, thought Jade. She got her notebook from the counter drawer. 'Just doing a stock check,' she told Netta.

Netta looked outraged. 'It's all on the database!'

I know, Jade mouthed, and winked at her. She found a pen and roamed the shop, pretending to make a tick in her notebook every so often.

'I'd have gone there first, but they aren't opening till half past nine. Definitely cheaper.'

'Yes. I do wonder about the markup in this place.'

'It is a bit fishy, and what with this business in the news… No smoke without fire, they say.'

'I heard they had a ding-dong in the shop. Over there, by the candles. I'm amazed it's allowed to open.'

Jade beat a retreat to the counter before she did or said something she might regret. 'Netta, I'm a bit worried about Stan,' she said. 'If you don't mind, I'll stay in the back room with him. Do we need to do anything more with those subscription boxes?'

'Seals and labels.' Netta got a sheaf of paper covered in sticky labels from the counter drawer and handed it to Jade. 'Stickers and address labels. You don't need to check the boxes, they're all the same. Make sure the tabs are tucked in on each side, then put a sticker over the front tab.'

'OK,' said Jade.

'Thanks,' said Netta. She didn't seem worried about Jade leaving her alone in the shop.

'Oh yes, just one thing.' Jade leaned in. 'Can you listen to the customers and make a note of anything they say which could be relevant to the murder?'

Netta's eyebrows shot up. 'Me?'

'You're right there. Here's my notebook.' Jade turned to a fresh page and put the notebook in front of Netta. 'See you in a bit. Tell you what, I'll bring you out a tea.'

Ten minutes later, Jade was bored. The cardboard tabs on the sides of the boxes were fiddly, and she couldn't get the stickers exactly straight. *It's what's inside that matters*, she told herself, but she wasn't convinced. Stan watched her movements from his basket, fascinated.

'I bet Fi wouldn't get lumbered doing a stupid job like this,' Jade told him. 'She'd get Zach or Nerys to do it, or Dylan. And if she did do it, I bet she'd put them on straight.' She sighed as she put a sticker on box number fifty. 'Not even halfway,' she said, disgusted.

Then a voice cut through the burbling beyond the door. 'Have you got nothing better to do than gossip? Really?'

'I just said Magical Moments was cheaper,' said a disgruntled female voice. 'No need to get your knickers in a twist, Sheena.'

'No, you didn't. I heard what you were saying. You're spreading rumours – *lies* – which could destroy someone's reputation.'

The other woman laughed. 'I'm only saying what people are thinking. Maybe they're too scared to say it, but I'm not. All that witchy stuff she does is an act. Otherwise why's she hiding, eh?'

'You should be ashamed of yourself!'

Jade crept to the door and peered through the keyhole. Standing with her back to Jade was a squat woman in a blue raincoat. Facing her, and looking as if lightning bolts might shoot from her eyes any moment, was one of the three witches. The first witch, Jade thought. 'I suppose you think gossiping's a bit of a laugh, but this is someone's business,' she said. 'And for your information, the stuff at Magical Moments is crap. I visited, out of curiosity. The only thing that place is good for is Halloween dress-up.'

'Takes a witch to know a witch, they say,' sneered the woman in the raincoat.

Sheena flung up her chin. 'Maybe it does, and I'm a white witch. A white witch who needs supplies. If you'll excuse me.' She walked round the shop gathering items, then took them to the counter.

'Wow,' breathed Jade.

The shop fell silent and a few people left. Jade went back to her subscription boxes. As she stuck a sticker on each box and smoothed it over the tab with her thumb, she imagined she was silencing the woman in the blue coat. Then she remembered Linzi Lawson and her face burned.

The job done at last, she went into the shop. 'Boxes are ready to go,' she told Netta. 'Will you sort out a collection?'

'OK.' said Netta.

Jade glanced around: no one was watching. 'Before you do,' she murmured, 'did you get anything from the customers?' She tapped the notebook, which was closed.

'What? Oh, no. I did try, but a woman caught me looking at her and frowned, so I decided I'd better not.'

'Never mind. It was only an idea.' Jade picked up the notebook and flipped through it till she found a page with a couple of lines in Netta's large round handwriting.

MM opening 9.30 am.

MM has three for two offer on incense cones. Also a loyalty card.

Jade closed the book. Honestly, could Netta think of nothing but bargains and sales? Practically everyone in the shop had come to gossip, and Netta had captured none of it.

She looked up and found Netta watching her. 'Well done,' she said. 'I'll let you get on. Want another brew?'

'Go on then,' said Netta. 'Can I have real tea this time?'

'There's hope for you yet,' said Jade, and went into the back. But as she went through the ritual of making tea, something nagged at her. It was like having a tiny piece of food caught between two teeth. *What is it?*

'Rrrerrfff?' Stan enquired, from his basket by the door.

'Does that mean walk?' Jade asked. 'Let me get this tea made and drunk, then we'll see about taking you outside.' She smiled at him. Then her gaze moved past him and she frowned.

Outside. The yard. More specifically, the bolt on the gate.

I didn't leave the gate unbolted – I know that. So who did?

And in her mind, there was an obvious answer.

CHAPTER 16

The Book Barge felt odd without Stan, but according to Jade, he was having a fine old time at Crystal Dreams.

Fi wondered if Jade would get a pet of her own after this, and if so, what she'd choose. A parrot, maybe. Or would that be too noisy?

'A mongoose,' suggested Marcus, when they video-called that morning. 'That would suit her better.'

'I'll tell her that.'

'Maybe not.'

'How's London?'

'Busy.' Marcus turned his phone and showed her the view from his hotel room: ancient and modern buildings huddled under grey skies, traffic rushing by. 'I'd better go. The Met have leads on the gang I think the influencer shoplifter's working for, but I don't want them taking over. This is my case and she's a Wyvernshire girl. Whatever she's got into, I want to see it through and make sure she's treated right.' He sighed. 'I gather nothing else has happened at your end.'

'No,' said Fi, showing Marcus the view from the boat rather than her face. 'Will you be back for the gig at the Feathers tomorrow?'

'The one where Dylan's band is the support act?' Marcus wrinkled his nose. 'Pop punk? I, er, hope so. After that . . . mine or yours?'

'Mine. The band are staying over at Alfie's following their musical triumph. We can listen to the river go by and . . . you know. Canoodle.'

'Can't wait.'

'Then hurry up and finish teaching the Met a thing or two about policing.'

'I will. And I'll make them keep their sticky mitts off my case. See you tomorrow.' Marcus blew a kiss and closed the call.

The day was as busy as the previous one but more manageable, since Zach was there. It was possible to build more short breaks into the morning and for each of them to take forty-five minutes for lunch.

When things are more normal, I must persuade Jade to get herself another assistant, thought Fi, as she made her way up to town. *Half her problem is being constantly exhausted.*

She considered collecting Stan before undertaking her mission, but he might as well stay where he was. She could fetch him when she reported back to Jade.

There was a *No dogs except guide dogs* sign on the door of Magical Moments and a disconsolate, shivering spaniel tied up outside when Fi arrived. She knew she'd been right to leave Stan with Jade. The windows had several special-offer posters plastered up. They were in primary colours, with a jolly font and lots of exclamation marks: not the sort of thing the town council liked, preferring muted tones to fit in with the historical buildings and cobbled streets.

Fi hadn't gone inside, mostly out of loyalty to Jade but also because its wares didn't interest her. She had, though, glanced in while passing. Now, something seemed different. But perhaps that was her imagination: a projection of the knowledge of Linzi's death and the assistant manager's reported grief.

I can check, she thought. *Magical Moments is part of a chain. They have a brand. Like Marcus said: cookie cutter.* She looked up the official website on her phone and compared the image of a typical store with what was in front of her. The Hazeby version was definitely different.

The shop had been refitted. The corporate standard for the shelves and counters was pine, as she recalled from previous forays. Now the furniture was white, although two pine cabinets stood near the till displaying fancy jewellery. Perhaps it had been too hard to find white replacements in a few days. In fact, it was astonishing they'd managed to change as much as they had, unless Linzi was part-way through the change when she was murdered. But why?

Signs hung over different parts of the shop, indicating what that section sold and somehow daring anything to be moved. Perhaps they'd been there before: Fi didn't know. Apart from a corporate photograph of Linzi on the counter, with an open book of condolence and a small posy of fabric flowers, everything was as impersonal and highly organised as a good supermarket. There was none of the quirky friendliness of Jade's shop, where, despite Netta's efforts, it was an adventure to wander round, with a good chance of coming across something unexpected.

You want to know exactly where things are in a supermarket, thought Fi, *but a magic shop should be like a bookshop – a place to browse, to get lost in and find hidden treasure. Of course the kids prefer Crystal Dreams. Marcus is right: Jade's regulars will come back.*

Apart from lack of personality, the other thing likely to drive away potential buyers was the staff's lack of interest. Fi peered at the mystical jewellery and gem-encrusted dragons in the locked cabinets and waited. One of the staff should have offered to unlock a cabinet for Fi and show her properly, but the two women at the counter ignored her. They were wearing black blouses patterned with spangles and purple sashes emblazoned with *Magical Moments* in curly pink script, from which tablets dangled. Fi presumed the tablets were for checking stock and wondered how much the shop assistants' necks ached at the end of the day.

A tall man in a suit paced the shop. From his black tie, patterned in spangles, and the way he was adjusting things on shelves, Fi assumed he was Harvey Batchelor, presumably now acting store manager.

The two assistants carried on chatting, ignoring Fi and everyone else. One of them had a mug of coffee, which she hugged with both hands while holding forth about how exhausted she was.

'Well, what with shifting everything around like we have been, Hannah, it's not surprising,' said her colleague. 'And dealing with SOCKY.'

'SOCO, Sonia,' said Hannah, authoritatively. 'Seen it on *24 Hours in Police Custody*.'

'Stupid name either way. Glad they didn't keep *us* for twenty-four hours. Linzi made us slog enough when she was alive, telling us that if this store wasn't a success we'd be toast. It's not fair that she even does it when she's dead.'

A third member of staff in a purple shirt and

spangled tie came out of a doorway that presumably led to the back area of the shop. He was carrying a smallish box of chocolates. 'We're nearly out of coffee and milk, Han,' he said. 'The police drank it like it was going out of fashion.'

'Thanks for telling me, Charlie.' Hannah clasped her mug tighter. 'Though the detective inspector drank hot water, which is plain unnatural. Talking of unnatural, Sonia – you've got plenty of your weird milk, haven't you?'

Sonia rolled her eyes. 'Oat milk isn't weird. I keep telling you, give veganism a go. It'll be good for your gut. You both look peaky.'

'Meh.' Charlie rubbed his stomach and pulled a face. 'Never worked out how you milk an oat.' He rattled the chocolates. 'Have a choccie. At least we didn't get these till after the police had gone, or they'd have scoffed them too. Oh no, they're not dairy free, so you can't! More for the rest of us!' He sniggered, then winced and wandered off to the *Gifts Under £5* section.

Fi glanced at the acting manager to see if he would deliver a reprimand, but Harvey Batchelor had stopped to inspect yet another shelf.

She gave up waiting to be served, went to the counter, and without removing her gloves, squiggled illegibly in the book of condolence. 'It must have been such a shock,' she said, in low, sympathetic tones. 'I'm after . . . a wishing-well water feature with mystical symbols. Ms Lawson said you'd have them in soon, but I wanted to offer my sympathy first. It was an unexpected way to die.'

'And the understatement of the year award goes to…' muttered Hannah.

'I'm not sure we do garden features,' said Sonia. 'I mean, we don't at this store. Maybe Linzi…' She tapped at the tablet that hung from her sash. 'Yes, it was a shock. Partly because, to be honest, we thought that if anything got her it would be overwork.'

'We were the ones being overworked,' muttered Hannah, staring into her mug.

'Don't speak ill of the dead,' said Sonia. 'Linzi was an ambitious woman: she wanted the Hazeby store to be top of the sales league. She said we could learn a lot from her. I'd rather be less ambitious and happy at home, myself. You're less likely to be murdered that way.'

'Do you think so?' said Fi. 'Wasn't Linzi happy at home?'

'Don't know if she had one,' said Hannah, leaning on the counter. 'She lived for business – literally, she'd moved into the flat above the shop – and she'd left her husband. I used to hear them arguing in the storeroom over selling the house. She wanted it on the market, but he wanted her to come back so they could try again.'

'Mr Lawson was in the storeroom?' said Sonia.

'No, he was on video calls. I never meant to listen, but I had to fetch stuff.'

'Every time they were talking?' said Fi.

'Oh yes – I couldn't help it. If we weren't on top of things, there'd be trouble. Not my fault I had to restock when she was video-calling.' Hannah burped delicately into her hand.

'May I help you, madam?' said a deep voice behind Fi, who jumped.

She turned to find Harvey Batchelor standing there. He looked expectant, his face serious and wan.

'She wants a garden feature,' said Sonia.

'Not *she*,' admonished Harvey. 'The customer, or the lady.'

'The lady customer wants a garden feature but I can't find one in our normal stock. Was Linzi ordering some?'

'Not that she told me.' Harvey assumed an apologetic expression and extracted a large phone from an inner pocket. 'Please explain what you mean, madam, and we— What's wrong, Hannah?'

Hannah had clapped one hand over her mouth. She waved the other before rushing through the door to the back.

Charlie ambled up. His face was a peculiar grey and covered in a fine sheen of sweat. 'What's up with Han? She looks sick. I don't feel too good myself.'

'To be honest,' said Harvey, 'neither do I.' He ran a finger round the inside of his collar.

'It's all those chocolates you've been scoffing,' said Sonia. 'Goodness knows what additives they've got in them. I'm glad I'm vegan.'

'I haven't had that many,' said Charlie. He peered into the box. 'Oh. But Hannah had lots too. How many have you had, Harv?'

'Mr Batchelor to you,' said Harvey. 'Only one.' He grimaced.

'I've had none and I'm fine,' said Sonia. 'Anyway, where did they come from? Did Hannah buy them? Or was it you, Mr Batchelor?'

'They were on the counter with a sympathy card this morning. Just before you arrived, Sonia,' said Charlie, licking his lips. 'A customer must have left them to cheer us up.'

'What was written on the card?' asked Fi.

'Nothing,' said Harvey. 'Just *In Sympathy* printed inside.' He motioned to Sonia to pass the card, which had a tombstone and flowers on the front.

Fi went cold. 'Don't touch that,' she said. 'Try and remember when you first saw the chocolates and who was here when they came. Something's not right. I think you've been poisoned.'

'Who are you, the police?' said Harvey. But he bit his lip as Charlie put the box down and rushed into the back, hand over mouth.

'Not even close,' said Fi. 'And I don't know what she'll say but so help me, I'm phoning Inspector Acaster. You'd better shut the shop.'

CHAPTER 17

'No, it's all right, Netta, you've done lots. I'll lock up. Go on, off you go.'

'I don't mind, honestly.'

'It's your first day back, and it's been busy.'

'If you're sure…' Netta got her things and left. The door closed quietly behind her.

Jade sighed, then locked the shop door and checked it twice before quickly cashing up. *It's been a good day, takings-wise. I wish everything was this good.* She transferred the money to bank bags and put them in a tote to take upstairs, then went through the connecting door which led to her flat and double-locked it. It wasn't robbers that worried her, though. It was something far, far worse.

Upstairs, she locked the cash in the small safe she had bought a few weeks ago, when there had been no rival magic shop in Hazeby and things had seemed wonderfully rosy. *Oh, to be back there, when all I had to worry about was how to expand Crystal Dreams still further.* She returned the safe key to its little plastic pouch, hid it at the bottom of her box of teabags, and decided a strong cup of tea was in order while she made sense of the latest mess.

Fi had finally arrived at Crystal Dreams at half past two. Jade had been about to make a smart remark, something like 'What time do you call this?' Then she saw Fi's face.

'Stan's in the back room,' she said, loud enough for everyone in the shop to hear. 'You needn't worry, he's been good as gold. I bet you've missed him.' She took Fi into the back room and closed the door. 'What's happened?' she murmured.

Fi went to Stan, who was sitting up in his basket, tail wagging. 'So you've been a good boy,' she said, at high volume. She beckoned Jade over and muttered 'Poisoned chocolates at Magical Moments.'

'*What?*'

'Keep your voice down. I went at one o'clock. The staff were distracted, chatting. Apparently, Linzi Lawson was rowing with her husband on video calls. It sounds as if they'd split up, but I don't know who started it. He wanted to try again, though: she didn't. The staff said Linzi overworked them. They didn't seem to like her.'

'OK, but what about these chocolates?'

'A box mysteriously appeared on the shop counter with a sympathy card this morning. The card was blank, with a picture of a tombstone and flowers. They tucked in, apart from one staff member who's vegan, and all felt sick. I rang Nina Acaster and told them not to touch the box or the card.'

'Good grief.' Jade felt a wave of sympathy for the Magical Moments staff. First a dictatorial manager, then a murder to contend with, and now the possibility that they were being targeted too.

'Have you got Stan's lead?' said Fi. 'I have to go. I've already had more than my break.'

'Yes, of course.' Jade unhooked the lead from the door and handed it to Fi. 'Thanks for letting me know. And if you want me to dog-sit again, I'm up for it. Stan was great. Weren't you?'

'Rrrerrfff!' said Stan, his tail a blur.

'Good stuff,' said Fi, but Jade could tell her heart wasn't in it. She looked weary, and a little as if she had eaten something which disagreed with her.

'Are you all right, Fi?' A horrible thought struck Jade. 'You didn't eat one of those chocolates, did you?'

'No, no. I really must go. We'll catch up soon.' Fi hurried through the shop and into the street.

Jade kept herself busy for the rest of the day: taking turns with Netta behind the counter, fetching stock from the shed without looking at the big green bin, and recording what she'd brought in her notebook for Netta to update on the database. All the time, she worried. Occasionally she glanced at Netta, serving confidently in a way she could never have done a year before. She remembered Netta's megawatt smile on the cover of *BizTech Retail News*. *Netta's going places*, she thought. *Do her plans include me?*

If I didn't unbolt the gate, it must have been Netta. No one else has access.

Netta wants to go big online and I don't. Reducing the success of the shop – or getting rid of me – would help her do that.

And when I asked her to gather evidence in the shop, she came up with nothing.

She glanced at Netta again, who was laughing at a customer's joke. *I don't want to believe it . . . but should I?*

The day's takings were no compensation for the bitter, frightening thoughts which had dogged Jade for most of the afternoon. Had Netta poisoned some chocolates – or put in something unpleasant but harmless – and got someone to sneak them into Magical Moments? What if, when analysed, the chocolates contained something which Crystal Dreams sold? 'It could be the end of me,' Jade whispered into her mug. *Perhaps I should start building a case. Not in my notebook, where Netta might see it—*

The doorbell rang and she jumped. That was her default response these days. *Maybe it's Fi, coming round to give me a bit more detail.* She wasn't sure whether that was good or not. *Or it could be him—*

Her blood froze in her veins. She peeped out of the front window and saw a head of longish, greyish hair.

Rick. Jade let out a slow breath and went downstairs.

'Hi,' said Rick. 'We haven't spoken properly for a while, so I thought I'd pop over and see how you are. How are things? Do you fancy a pre-dinner drink?' His hopeful expression was almost more than Jade could bear. 'Or we could get a bite to eat if you haven't cooked, or—'

'I'm really tired, Rick,' she said. 'The shop was busy today, and with everything else…' *The surprise arrival of my ex-boyfriend and Hugo's dad, a murder I'm implicated in, not knowing if my assistant's trying to get rid of me…* 'Could we do it another time?'

Rick frowned. 'We could, but—'

Jade's phone buzzed and she checked it. Hugo, on video call. *Oh no.* 'I have to go,' she muttered, and closed the door.

She answered the phone as she was going upstairs. 'Hi, I was at the door,' she said. 'Give me a moment.'

'OK, Mummy.' Hugo sounded amused, and she relaxed a little. Then again, she had never been good at knowing what he was thinking. He'd always been able to hide his emotions. *Is that because of something I did?*

She entered her flat and sat on the edge of the sofa. 'Right, I'm in.' She braced herself for whatever was coming next.

Hugo grinned at her. 'You look as if I'm about to pronounce sentence, Mummy.'

'Do I?' Jade attempted to look calm.

'First of all, I'm not angry and you're not in trouble. Not exactly.'

Oh heck. 'That's a good start,' said Jade. She gazed longingly at the mug sitting on her worktop, waiting to be filled with tea.

'I think you know what I'm going to say next.'

'Not the foggiest,' said Jade. 'Out with it.'

'I had a phone call,' said Hugo. 'From someone saying he was my dad. He talked about you a bit, and how he happened to find you. He asked if we could meet and I said OK. So we did, this afternoon, in a coffee shop in Oxford.'

'Uh huh.' Jade paused, wondering what on earth to say. 'Um, how did it go?'

Hugo smiled. 'We got on really well. I had no idea he worked in tech. That probably explains how he found me so easily.'

That, and your name being in that flaming article, thought Jade.

'He wasn't anything like I expected,' said Hugo.

'Not that you've said much about him, but I thought he'd be a bit of a chancer and he didn't seem that way at all. He was . . . like a dad. How I imagine one, anyway.' He took a drink from a chunky cream mug with a big navy H emblazoned on the side in curlicue lettering, and Jade felt even thirstier. 'I don't know why you two didn't... He was nice. Considerate.'

'He's changed a lot,' Jade said curtly.

'Yes, he said he was a bit of a good for nothing till he pulled himself together.' Hugo put his mug down. 'He said you didn't want to speak to him.'

'No, I didn't,' said Jade. 'What's past is past, and there's no point digging it up.'

'Mmm,' said Hugo. 'You won't like this, Mummy, but I think you should give him a chance.'

'I'm seeing Rick, in case you've forgotten.' *Who I just shut the door on. For all I know, he's still standing outside.* Jade rubbed the skin between her eyebrows. *No wonder I keep getting headaches.*

'I don't mean like that, Mummy. I mean that maybe you two should talk and work through whatever happened. Maybe go to counselling?'

'I'm not going to counselling with Daz!' Jade cried. 'I left him for a reason. And no, I'm not going to talk about it. I don't *want* to talk about it. I'm a grown woman, so I don't have to.' Hugo gazed at her steadily and she sighed. 'I don't mind you meeting him, but don't expect me to.'

'OK, Mummy. I think you'd be happier if you worked through it, but it's up to you. And you'll have to get used to the idea of me meeting up with him.' He glanced at his watch. 'Got to go. I'm guesting on a crime podcast tonight and we're due to record in ten minutes.'

'Enjoy your evening,' Jade said, on autopilot.

'Bye, Mummy.' He ended the call.

Jade got up and finally allowed the mug to fulfil its destiny. *Poor Hugo. All these years, I've kept his dad from him. Of course they get on. What would his life have been like if I'd stayed? Let Daz take care of me? Run the house and looked after Hugo while Daz brought home the bacon?*

A sudden, horrible thought occurred to her. Darren the hotshot tech whizz would be a catch. Surely he had married and had a family. If he had kids, they had probably had all the chances and opportunities Hugo had missed out on.

A tear rolled down her cheek and she wiped it away before it had the chance to plop into her mug. 'Too late now,' she whispered, with a lump in her throat.

CHAPTER 18

Fi was at least as tall as Nina, but when the latter arrived at Magical Moments to investigate the possible poisoning, minutes after it had been reported, Fi had immediately felt as if the other woman was leaning down to reprimand her. It was both irritating and intimidating. The feeling grew worse when, in a few sharp words, Nina gave her opinion on Fi being there in the first place.

'Falconer being away doesn't give you carte blanche to play detective,' Nina whispered, while the staff were taken away by a constable to make informal statements. 'Don't think I don't know why you're here. This place is competition for Crystal Dreams, where the body was found. And Jade Fitch is your sidekick – or are you hers? I keep expecting to find the pair of you in masks and capes.' Nina straightened up and sniggered at her own joke.

'I came in to sign the book of condolence, like most of the town,' said Fi. 'I—'

'How kind. Anyway, time to head off in your CrystalBookmobile, or whatever you superheroes drive. I'll be round later to take your statement.'

Fi hadn't been able to face telling Jade what Nina had said when she went to collect Stan, and as the afternoon wore on, the moment to do so passed. Back at the Book Barge, she worked on autopilot, waiting for Nina to turn up or for Marcus to ring and reprimand her too. Neither happened, but she took her anxiety out on everyone in her path, and Dylan in particular. To be fair, Dylan walked into Fi's path ready to dispute anything and everything.

Nina still hadn't appeared by six o'clock, when the theatre rang to ask Dylan to work for a short time that evening as well as the following morning. He didn't want to.

'Fine,' snapped Dylan, after an argument which had gone on for what felt like hours. 'I'll go to the theatre before going out with my friends. It would be nice if you supported me like other parents do, but—'

'I do! But you have to honour your commitments, and it's only—'

'All you care about is the shop and Marcus and Jade and telling people I work at the theatre, cos it sounds more cultured than a band.'

In his basket, Stan whined softly and put his paws

over his nose.

'None of that's true,' said Fi. 'How dare you?'

'Don't expect me back early. It's Friday night and I'm not ten.'

'Someone was murdered the other day,' Fi countered. 'I'd rather—'

'Someone's always being murdered in Hazeby these days. There's a bunch of us and we'll be indoors. Anyway, we're not old shopkeepers like the victim.'

'She wasn't—'

'Do you want to argue, or do you want me to go to the theatre?'

'The theatre wants you to go,' said Fi. 'Could you show some respect, please? They said if you work half an hour now, you'll work less tomorrow morning. That's good, isn't it?'

Her phone started vibrating, juddering across the table.

The anger on Dylan's face became revulsion. 'If that's Marcus, I'm out of here. I'm not listening to two old people slobbering over each other.' Before she could retort, he stormed off.

Fi put her hand on the phone to stop it moving. The vibration under her palm wound her up even more. *Urgent! Urgent! Answer! Answer! Now! NOW!* She wondered whether the phone would disintegrate if she flung it against the wall, or just make a hole and fall to the ground, still ringing.

It stopped.

Unwilling to check the display and see who'd been calling, because she was uncertain who would be worst, Fi argued with herself instead.

You should have discussed the theatre thing with Dylan more calmly.

Why should I always be the reasonable one?

He's a teenager. You're supposed to be the adult.

I'm sick of being the adult.

The phone rang again. Running her hand over her face, in the hope that it would somehow transform her anxiety into calm, Fi picked it up.

It was her mother. 'Hello, darling. Busy?'

'I was seeing Dylan off. He's up to his ears in things at the moment. None of them schoolwork.'

Her mother laughed. 'You were the same when you were in the lower sixth. We had to ban you from going to parties and make you knuckle down.'

'Did you? I don't remember.'

'That's because you like to think of yourself as a goody-two-shoes. Although you are really, aren't you? Dylan is, too. Try doing the same with him.'

'Huh,' said Fi. '*You* do it.'

'Move here and I will.'

'Teenage strops aside, we're fine where we are, Mum.'

'Are you?' said Fi's mother. 'No one's been

murdered in this town since 1954, which is more than I can say for Hazeby-on-Wyvern. Did you think I wouldn't hear about it? *And* the murder in 1954 was a *crime passionnel.*'

'Does that make it OK?'

'Well, no. But none of the crimes in Hazeby were crimes of passion.'

Maybe this one is, thought Fi, remembering the gossip about Linzi and Joe Lawson.

Her mother's voice changed tone. 'Come on, Fi, move to Normandy. There'd be a lot of red tape to go through at first, but the Book Barge would become part of the gîte complex. We'd be a family concern, following a dream together.'

Fi sighed. Murders aside, she was following a dream – but it was her own dream. She didn't want it to be subsumed into her mother's. 'Not yet, Mum. Dylan's got school and M— my friends are here.'

'You were going to say Marcus.' Her mother chuckled, but there was a little sadness in it. 'At least he can protect you from whoever's responsible for the latest murder. I'm looking forward to meeting him properly. But please promise you won't dismiss France.'

'No, Mum.'

'And keep safe, Marcus notwithstanding.'

'Yes, Mum. Love you.'

'Love you too.'

Fi put the phone on the table, ran her hands through her hair, then pre-empted her former mother-in-law Annie by messaging her.

Hi. I expect you've heard there's been another murder. Please don't worry about Dylan and me. We're fine and it's being investigated properly. I'm sure you'd like to offer to take Dylan, but he's busy with school and theatre and he wouldn't want to let his friends down at the gig tomorrow night. Looking forward to seeing you when you come to watch Blithe Spirit, by which time I'm sure the murder will be a distant memory.

If you're sure, came the reply. *But if you change your mind, please don't be scared to say so.*

She was tempted to tell Annie to come and fetch her grandson and keep him, given the way Dylan was behaving. The thought of Annie in ninja mode, trying to force Dylan to leave his friends and social life then fight off a murderer, made Fi grin. Then her phone rang yet again.

She expected it to be Annie, with a barrage of hints and suggestions, but the display said *N Acaster*. Fi's face burned, remembering their earlier conversation. Nina couldn't even be bothered to turn up. She was simply phoning.

'I've been waiting for you to visit,' she snapped.

'No time,' said Nina. 'Tell me what you think you know.'

'Should we be doing this over a mobile network?'

'As I said, no time to visit.'

Fi counted to ten, then began. 'From the way the staff were behaving, I was sure those chocolates were poisoned. If I was wrong, I apologise for wasting police time.'

'You were right, and you didn't.' The words were clipped. Then Nina's voice softened. 'So thank you. And no one has anything worse than a slight stomach upset.'

'I'm so glad.'

'How else can you help?'

'The interior decor of that shop has been changed.'

'Uh-huh.' It was hard to be sure if Nina was agreeing, or taking note of something she hadn't realised.

'My impression was that gossip is more important to the staff than customer service,' said Fi. 'I would have told you that earlier, but you were too busy telling me to go away. If it's not too late, perhaps that gossip's worth listening to.'

'I'll look into it.' Nina sniffed and there was a sound like a notebook being snapped shut. 'No harm done, thankfully. But I stand by what I said earlier. Please don't be a hero.'

'Glad to help,' said Fi, between gritted teeth. 'How's the case going?'

'It's following the proper, reliable procedures,' said

Nina. 'It's a well-worn path and we're experts. Thanks for your input, but stick to bookselling. Goodbye.'

Fi slammed down the mobile, tempted to turn it off. The next person to phone would probably be Marcus, asking why she'd been shopping for a water feature when she lived on a river and her garden was the potted plants on the deck. Then he'd tell her to back off or ask if Jade had put her up to it, as if Fi couldn't make her own decisions. The only thing that would be worse was if he repeated Nina's jokes about superheroes.

It wouldn't be so bad if Jade and I were actually getting somewhere, she thought. *Is the gossip about Linzi's marriage relevant?*

Joe Lawson was the obvious suspect, but he and Linzi had been at the shouting stage of a separation. Would she really have confided in him about a rival business which might affect her chance of climbing the career ladder that had destroyed their marriage? It seemed unlikely.

Or was Crystal Dreams a coincidence? thought Fi, with rising hope. *Perhaps Joe was lugging Linzi's body along that alley and opened the first unbolted gate he came to. But then...*

The hope dissolved into chill misery. Fi closed her eyes and visualised the scene. Could anyone carry a dead body down the alley without someone seeing them? Was Linzi dead before the murderer took her there, or had she been murdered in the yard? The police still hadn't published that level of detail. If so, was it relevant whose yard it was? And why had the gate been open?

'Rrrerrfff.' Stan was looking up with his head on one side and the tiniest of doggy frowns.

'You agree, don't you?' said Fi, lifting him into her lap for a cuddle. 'There's no way Jade would murder anyone, and if she ever did, she'd have the sense not to do it on her own turf. So that goes back to the culprit framing her. Who would do that, and why?'

None of it made sense.

Her phone buzzed over and over again.

Why don't you think about it? said her mother.

I've finished at the theatre. Will you stop nagging now? said Dylan.

If you've forgotten anything, be sure you tell me as soon as you remember, said Nina.

I'm busy, let's talk tomorrow, said Marcus.

No kisses. No pleases or thank yous.

'Rrrerrff.' Stan nudged Fi's hand with his nose. In his own way, he was bossier than Nina, her mother, Dylan and Marcus put together, but Fi didn't care.

'You're right,' she said. 'They can all wait. It's time for a walk. A long one.'

CHAPTER 19

The next morning, the news about the poisoning at Magical Moments was all over Crystal Dreams. Every customer, it seemed, had heard. Their sister lived next door to one of the shop assistants, or their husband worked with one of the shop assistants' husbands, or one of the couple who ran the corner shop had been there when it happened. Not for the first time, Jade wondered if Hazeby-on-Wyvern was actually a huge network of relatives and acquaintances to which, as a newcomer, she was not connected.

The story was online, too. *SUSPECTED POISONING DEALS ANOTHER BLOW TO TROUBLED SHOP*, shouted one headline. *MURDER SHOP POISONING*, screamed another publication with fewer words to spare.

'It's awful,' Netta said to the customer she was serving, usually a cheerful woman, who had held up the queue for several minutes with various speculations on what had taken place at Magical Moments. Jade, restocking the small cauldrons, had paused to listen. 'Those poor people. You expect work to be a safe place.'

'You do,' said the customer. 'And if a box of chocolates appears on *your* counter and you don't know where it's from, I hope you and Jade have more sense than to eat them.'

'Of course we do!' said Netta, though Jade saw her shudder. She packed the customer's purchases in a bag and set it on the counter. 'There you are. Cash or card?'

The customer produced her credit card and touched it to the reader.

As Netta waited for the transaction to process, she sipped from her mug of camomile tea. But she didn't swallow. She paused, an odd expression on her face.

'Is there a problem?' said the customer.

Netta shook her head and lifted the mug again, but Jade noticed she still hadn't swallowed. Presumably, she had gently spat her mouthful of tea back in the mug.

Netta put the mug down, a little further away. 'No, that's gone through fine,' she said. 'Jade, could you take over? Bathroom break.' And she hurried off.

'It's unfortunate for the other shop, having to close again,' said the next customer, as he put a book on modern herbalism on the counter. 'Nothing wrong in you making hay while the sun shines, though.'

'No, I suppose not,' said Jade. But her mind was elsewhere. On Netta, who had just spat out her tea in front of a customer then rushed to the bathroom. *There's nothing wrong with that tea: I made it myself. Is she trying to insinuate...?*

Netta returned a few minutes later and retrieved her mug. 'Do you want a brew, Jade?'

'I'm all right, thanks,' said Jade. *Two can play at that game.* 'You haven't finished that one.'

'It's cold,' said Netta, after a tiny pause. 'It's not as nice when it's cold.'

'It's pretty disgusting when it's warm,' Jade replied. 'But you do you.'

'I will, thanks,' said Netta, and disappeared into the back room.

Good riddance, thought Jade.

The chatter and gossip continued all morning. By half past eleven the same few facts had been trotted out so many times, usually with the same half-baked theories attached to them, that Jade could have used the Magical Moments poisoning as her specialist round on *Mastermind*. And she was still on the till, since Netta had suddenly remembered some subscriptions admin which required both her laptop and peace and quiet in the back room. *If I hear one more daft theory...*

'I don't think there was any human intervention,' said a blonde woman with a bubble perm. 'It was a punishment for meddling with the supernatural. The only thing I can't decide was whether it came from above' – she leaned forward – '*or below.*'

'If you'll excuse me a moment,' said Jade. She opened the back-room door and Netta nearly jumped out of her chair. To be fair, she had been absorbed in a spreadsheet. However, Jade wondered if Netta's reaction was reasonable, or the sign of a guilty conscience.

'Sorry to interrupt,' she said blandly, 'but would you mind taking over? I'm starving, and the speculation is getting on my nerves.'

'I'm in the middle of something.'

'It'll keep. Just make sure you save it.' Jade pulled the door to. 'Frankly, I'm desperate for a break. I'll actually be pleased when Magical Moments reopens and some of this lot stop bothering us.'

Netta frowned. 'That's not very business minded.'

'No, but they're doing my head in. It's quietened down, anyway, so you can carry on between customers.' Without waiting for a response, Jade reopened the door. 'I'm on early lunch today,' she announced to the shop. 'Netta will look after you.' Behind her, she heard the laptop close, accompanied by low muttering. She definitely felt lighter as she collected her bag and shut the shop door.

Fresh air and a proper break, she thought as she strode along. *That's what I need.* But as she stood in the queue at Betsy's, as she walked to the river with her bacon roll and cup of tea, and as she sat on a bench, munching and watching the world go by, Netta was in her mind. Netta, making out that her tea tasted funny. Netta, working secretly on her laptop and jumping when Jade came in. Netta, unbolting the gate—

You don't know that.

It must have been her. The only reason to leave the gate open is to cause trouble. Either by someone breaking in and stealing stock or money, or by something like this happening.

She wouldn't.

Netta's smart. And I won't let her go as far as she wants to with the business.

She could leave and set up on her own. That wouldn't be half as risky as what you're suggesting she's doing.

And what would she use for capital? Netta's what, twenty? Even if she's saved half of what I've paid her, that wouldn't get her very far.

She could take out a loan.

Jade recalled what Netta had said about deciding against university once she looked at the costs. *Or she could push me out.* She had a hazy idea of how that might work. *I don't know whose name is on all the online stuff. Netta may be able to claim a stake in the business.* She shivered. *What a fool I've been. Again.*

She finished her bacon roll, though she had no memory of actually eating it, screwed up the greasy paper bag and dropped it in the bin. Then she drained her cup and executed a slam dunk. *Get rid of the junk*, she thought. *That's what I need to do.*

She got up and marched to Crystal Dreams, firmly on the warpath. *First, I'll check what Netta's been up to online, then I'll tell her what's what. I'm not having someone pull the rug from under my feet.*

When she opened the shop door, Netta's wary expression set her teeth on edge. Luckily, the shop was quiet. 'I can tell you're glad to see me,' she said, hanging up her bag.

'That man's here,' said Netta. 'I told him you were on your lunch, but he said he'd wait. I put him in the back room.'

'What did you do that for?' Jade stormed across the shop and flung open the door. Darren was sitting at the table, scrolling on his phone. He looked up at her with a conciliatory expression. 'What are you doing here?' she demanded. 'I don't want to see you. Or speak to you.'

'I've come to clear the air.'

'Really? Well, the best way you can clear the air in this room is by getting out. I know you've visited Hugo. If you two want to have cosy chats, that's fine.

Just stay away from me.'

He said nothing.

'Go on, get out! Go!'

Slowly, Darren put his phone in his pocket and stood up. 'I'm sorry it's come to this,' he said. He walked through the shop and out, closing the door quietly.

Netta's eyes were like saucers. 'Who is that guy?'

'Never you mind,' snapped Jade. 'I'm not in the mood for questions, so if you want a lunch break, now's a good time. Oh yes, and before you go, give me the password for your laptop and the login for the online stuff. I need to check something.'

Netta's eyebrows shot up. 'That's my laptop.'

'Which you're using for work stuff connected with my business. So I need access to it.'

Netta folded her arms. 'It's my laptop, with my personal stuff on it. I can set up a login to the online store for you, but you can't use mine. That's bad practice.'

'So is acting as if I might have poisoned your tea in front of a customer. So is keeping your boss out of the loop with regard to her own business.' Jade's brain told her that showing Netta she was on to her was a terrible strategy, but she couldn't stop herself. 'So is unbolting the gate, for reasons known only to yourself.'

'What?' Netta had turned dead white. 'What are

you saying?'

'You heard.'

Netta said nothing. Jade could almost hear the cogs spinning as she pieced everything together and realised she was on borrowed time. Then Netta blinked and a tear rolled down her cheek. 'I can't believe you'd think that,' she choked out. 'I've worked so hard for you, and this is what I get. You've never cared about looking at the online stuff before, so why now?' She gazed at Jade with frightened eyes. 'Are you trying to frame me?' she whispered.

I want to believe her, thought Jade. But something held her back.

'I even returned to work after finding a dead body,' Netta sobbed, 'and you're accusing me of plotting behind your back!' Still crying, she got her bag from its peg.

Jade wondered if she could be mistaken. 'Netta, I—'

'For all I know, that guy I put in the back room is a hitman!'

'*What?*'

The shop door creaked and they both turned.

The smile on Rick's face faded. 'What's going on?' he asked, looking from Jade to Netta. 'Has something happened?'

'Why don't you ask your girlfriend,' said Netta. 'And you can ask her about her mystery man, too.'

She flounced out, slamming the door.

Rick watched her go. Slowly, he faced Jade, and his puzzled expression had become one of realisation. *He thinks I've been cheating on him. Even Rick thinks the worst of me.*

My business is failing, I'm under suspicion of murder, my own son is on his father's side, and I've lost the only man I ever trusted.

Without a word, Jade got her bag.

'Jade, talk to me,' Rick muttered.

'No point,' she said. 'And don't follow me.'

She walked round him and left the shop, not bothering to close the door. *I've had enough. I tried, but it didn't work. It never works.*

She took a side street, heading for the patch of waste ground where Bertha was parked. *Time to move on.*

CHAPTER 20

Marcus rang Fi early, but if he'd heard about the poisoning, he didn't mention it.

'I'll be back in plenty of time for the gig,' he said. 'I'm looking forward to cuddling up afterwards and *not* talking about crime.'

Fi sighed inwardly. Assuming he didn't have a go at her because she'd got involved in Nina's investigation, she wanted to confide in him about Linzi's murder and ask his views. She could only hope he'd change his mind.

Dylan appeared for breakfast in a better mood than the day before, absorbed enough cereal and toast for three people, and after ruffling Fi's hair, left the boat.

The day rattled by. Nerys had some time off, leaving Fi and Zach to manage. Business was brisk. Several local customers gossiped about the poisoning. Many bought books on identifying toxic plants, or novels such as *Strong Poison* and *Sparkling Cyanide*. It was both bizarre and macabre.

Fi wondered whether Jade was experiencing similar, but there was no time to message. There was barely time for a snack at lunchtime.

Presumably Jade was just as busy, because Fi's phone remained silent until she was serving a customer and Zach was showing another to the section they wanted. Fi didn't recognise the number, and besides, her customer was shoving a selection of books and a handful of banknotes into her hands. It was probably a cold call, and if not, the caller would ring back if it was important.

When Zach returned with his customer, Fi left the phone on the counter while she walked around the shop, tidying up. If it rang, Zach would answer if the caller was a supplier, or bring it over if the call looked personal.

The shop became quiet, but Fi's mind whirred. She pondered the customers who had bought books on poisoning. Were they protecting themselves or getting ideas? Was one of her customers the murderer, playing a double bluff? The thought unnerved her.

'Crippen,' breathed a deep voice in her ear. She jumped, nearly knocking the display of sundries on the floor. A man in his early fifties stood beside her, smiling blandly. He wore jeans and a bomber jacket that was a little too small. His longish hair was unstyled and a little greasy. She didn't recognise him. Could this be the man who'd been pestering Jade? Could he be...

'Crippen,' he repeated.

'Um, yes?'

'What's the best book on him?' The man leaned a little closer. 'You know. Poisoned his wife and hid her remains. Grisly. Aconite, wasn't it?'

Fi shook herself. 'I'm not sure. Non-fiction or fiction?'

'I'm not keen on made-up stuff,' said the man. 'I like facts. What you got?'

'Let's see.' Fi led the customer to the true-crime shelves where, as it turned out, there were two books on Crippen.

'Is that all?'

'It's all I have,' said Fi. 'Do you want something specific? I could order it in for you.'

'What others are there?'

Repressing a sigh, Fi collected her tablet from the counter and took it to the man. An online search revealed a mind-boggling number of books. 'If I send you this link, you can look through what's available to order.'

'I don't like the internet. Can't you tell me what each one's about?'

Fi wondered why she'd ever gone into bookselling. She was about to lead him to the seating area when

Rick rushed down the steps.

'This man – Jade's skedaddled – the shop's open and no one's there… Bertha – she— I tried to phone…' Rick stopped to take a breath.

'Rick, can you go up on deck?' said Fi. 'I'll join you in a second.'

She ushered the customer to the counter and handed Zach the tablet. 'Let me leave you with my internet whizz,' she said. 'Zach, the gentleman would like a brief summary of each of these books on Crippen.' She mouthed *Sorry,* then ran up the steps.

Rick was pacing, hugging himself against the cold. Fi put her hand on his arm. 'Is Jade all right?'

'I don't know. I don't think so.'

Fi gasped.

'I mean, she seems OK physically, but I'm worried about her state of mind. I hoped she'd called you.'

'She hasn't. What's happened?'

'I popped into the shop and found her and Netta having a row. Then Netta said something about Jade having a mystery man and stormed out. I asked Jade to talk to me and *she* stormed out. She said not to follow, but—'

'You did. Good.'

'I couldn't stop her driving off in Bertha.' Rick drew another breath. 'I went back to the shop in case Netta had returned and could explain. She hadn't. And there wasn't a man around. So I wondered if I'd misheard. Then I remembered I'd seen a man coming out of Jade's shop as I was locking up. He looked miserable.'

Fi felt her tension increase. 'Was it the man who's downstairs?'

'I— Hang on.' Rick went down to the shop, then returned. 'Nope. The man I saw was smart and bald. I rang you, and when you didn't answer I turned the sign to *Closed* and came here. This man…'

'Jade's not cheating on you, Rick,' said Fi.

'Like I thought she would!' He stared. 'She's secretive, not dishonest. But if he's hurting her…' His hands clenched.

'I think he's hassling her. That's all I know. She won't tell me any more.'

'She hasn't told me anything. I wish she'd talk to me. I wish she'd trust me.'

'Me too,' said Fi. 'Hopefully, she'll drive for a bit to get her feelings out of her system, then return. I'll get my phone and message her.'

The customer who'd wanted a Crippen book emerged from the shop, waving a paper bag. 'I bought one and I've got another on order. Great service. Wouldn't have got that in a chain store.'

Fi let him pass with a smile, chiding herself for her initial reaction to him. There were no potential customers in sight. She could close early and—

'Hold on,' she said to Rick. 'Is Crystal Dreams

unlocked?'

'What else could I do? The only people with keys are Jade and Netta. Unless you have a set. And you weren't answering your phone.'

'We'll go there now. I don't have keys but at least we can make it secure. I'll get my phone and tell Zach to close up.'

A few minutes later they were inside Crystal Dreams, with a chair wedged against the door handle. There was no response when Fi called Jade, though if she was driving, that was to be expected. Netta, however, did answer. Fi put the phone on speaker.

'Has she made you act as go-between, Fi?' Netta's voice was full of tears and she sniffed wetly. 'Is she sorry for what she said? I can't believe she'd think that, let alone say it. I thought we were friends.'

'I don't know what's happened,' said Fi, as gently as she could, 'but I'm sure it's a misunderstanding. Jade has driven off in Bertha and we're worried about her. Also, Crystal Dreams is unlocked.'

'She's done what?'

'She wasn't thinking straight,' said Fi. 'Maybe she forgot to lock up.'

'I don't mean the shop, I mean going off in Bertha. You shouldn't drive upset.' There was another wet sniff and a small sob. 'I-I hope she's all right. I'll come down and lock up.'

'Thanks, Netta. Jade's got a lot on her mind. I

think this man has frightened her.'

There was a brief silence. 'Not frightened,' said Netta. 'He worries her. He knows Hugo – at least, I think that's what she meant. I haven't asked Hugo. But that doesn't give her the right to accuse me of framing her. Or to try and frame *me*.'

'What?' Fi stared at Rick, who looked nonplussed. 'Netta, everyone needs to sit down and talk this through. First, though, we must secure the shop and find Jade.' She rang off and video-called Hugo, glad that he'd given her his number 'in case Mummy gets in bother,' as he put it.

He answered on the first ring. 'What's she done?'

'She's gone off somewhere,' said Rick. 'A man's been hassling her, and—'

'He hasn't hassled anyone,' said Hugo. 'He just wanted her permission to talk to me.'

'You?' said Rick.

'He's called Darren Hartley and he's my dad. Didn't she tell you?' Hugo rolled his eyes. 'Of course not.'

Fi and Rick exchanged glances. Fi couldn't believe it hadn't occurred to her that the mystery man from Jade's distant past could be Hugo's father. If it hadn't been for the murder, that would have been the first thing she'd have thought of. But why did Jade have to be so defensive about it? Fi would never have judged her.

'So that's why she's been pushing me away,' said Rick. 'Like I'd care. It's ancient history.'

'Not so much of the ancient, please,' said Hugo. He didn't sound as light-hearted as his words.

'Sorry, mate. Hang on . . . have you only just found out?'

'Yes. Mummy never said who my father was and I gave up asking. We were happy, she's a great mum, and I thought my dad didn't care. Turns out he didn't know where we were and he's managed to track her – and therefore me – down.' Hugo looked pensive. 'Mummy doesn't want anything to do with him.'

Rick let out a relieved sigh.

'And you, Hugo?' said Fi.

'It sort of completes a puzzle for me. And he's OK – nice, actually. Wait, did you say Mummy's gone off?'

'Yes,' said Fi, 'and we're worried. I thought she might drive round the lanes then come back, but there's no sign of her. She could be miles away.'

'I can track her,' said Hugo.

'How?' said Rick.

'I enabled Find my iPhone on her mobile in case she ever, well, did what she's doing now. Hang on.' Hugo looked down, presumably tapping at his phone.

Someone banged on the door: Netta, hammering to be let in. Rick admitted her and Fi gave a very brief update while they waited.

Hugo looked up. 'OK... Mummy's about five miles from you, heading for Mistleby.'

'Really?' said Fi. 'I thought she'd be out of the county.'

'Not at three miles an hour,' said Hugo. 'Either she can't get Bertha out of first gear or she's walking. Will you go and get her?'

'Yes,' said Fi. 'Thanks, Hugo. I'll let you and Netta know as soon as we find her.'

She and Rick left Netta to lock up, then headed off in Fi's car. Two miles out of town they passed Bertha, abandoned on the narrow verge. Three miles on, they saw a tall figure trudging along, head down, hands deep in pockets. They passed her, then pulled up. Fi got out, rushed to Jade and threw her arms around her.

'Bertha ran out of petrol.' Jade slumped in Fi's embrace. 'I can't even run away properly.'

Rick pulled her gently from Fi and enveloped her in a bear hug. 'Bertha's a good car,' he said. 'She knows that if you're going to run, you should run to us. We'll always be here.'

'But—'

'Never mind but.' He kissed the top of her head. 'Fi and I know about Darren Hartley.'

'But—'

'Did you think we'd care? It's OK, Jade. It's OK.'

Jade's head lifted from Rick's chest and she looked

at Fi, her eyes full of tears.

'He's right,' said Fi. 'You're running the wrong way. Come home, and tell us what's really wrong.'

CHAPTER 21

'Come on,' said Rick, 'let's get you home.'

Jade shuddered, remembering her confrontation with first Darren, then Netta in the shop. Even upstairs, in the flat, she would think of it... 'Can we stay out for a bit?'

'Of course we can,' said Fi. 'Shall we drive somewhere quiet and get a cup of tea? It's quite a nice day for October.'

Jade wasn't sure why Fi was being so kind when, yet again, she had pulled Fi away from her work and into another crisis. Not to mention Rick, who she'd just walked out on. 'I'm sorry,' she whispered, the words catching in her throat.

Rick rubbed her arm. 'To the Fimobile.' He walked her to Fi's car. 'Shall we sit in the back, Fi?'

'I'll play chauffeur,' said Fi.

Fi found a place to turn, then drove towards the

village. They passed Bertha, squatting forlornly on the verge. 'Don't worry,' said Fi. 'We can pick up a petrol can and sort her out later. Right now, I'm more worried about you.'

'I'm fine,' murmured Jade.

'Mmm,' said Rick, and squeezed her hand. 'I wouldn't go that far.' But he left it at that, for which Jade was grateful.

Fi drove towards Hazeby, then took a left before they entered the town. A few minutes later, she pulled into a small, gravelled parking area. 'The river's here,' she said, 'and a little café with benches outside.'

They walked along the winding path, passing through trees to a grassy area which gave onto the riverbank. The café was little more than a wooden hut painted duck-egg blue, with a couple of tables inside and picnic benches in front.

'It's busy in summer,' said Fi. 'It'll be quiet now. Tea?'

'Please,' said Jade and Rick, together.

'Anything else? Toast?'

'No thanks,' said Jade. Keeping the tea down felt enough of a task.

'Actually, I wouldn't mind,' said Rick. 'I'll get these, if you want.'

That means he's missed lunch, thought Jade. *Fi probably has too. Why do they put up with me?*

Fi waved away the offer. 'You decide where to sit.'

She went into the café. Jade imagined what Fi might say to the server. *Three teas please, some toast, and a side order of patience for me as I deal with my flaky friend.* Though whether Fi would still be her friend...

'Jade?' Rick was looking at her expectantly. 'Is this one OK?' He was pointing to the picnic bench nearest the river.

'Yes, it's fine.'

He sat down. Jade took the place opposite.

Fi returned with two large navy mugs, steaming gently. 'The bags are still in,' she said. 'I wasn't sure how strong you liked yours, Rick, and I know Jade likes a builder's brew. Toast's just doing.' She wandered back to the café.

Jade sipped cautiously from her mug, which brought Netta to mind. She put the mug down as if it had burned her and burst into tears.

'What is it?' Rick ran round the table and gathered her in his arms. 'What's wrong?'

'Everything!' Jade wailed.

'It may seem that way, but I'm sure it isn't as bad as you think.'

'It's probably worse.'

Rick stroked her hair, saying nothing, and gradually Jade's sobs abated. Gently, she freed herself from Rick as Fi arrived with her tea and a plate of toast. 'Get it while it's hot,' she said and sat down, taking a piece.

'Don't mind if I do,' said Rick. 'Jade?'

Jade shook her head. Toast would probably choke her: she was barely able to speak as it was. She had another try at her tea, and managed not to start crying again.

'I suppose you want to know about Daz,' she said. 'He goes by Darren now, but he was Daz when we were going out.'

Rick put a hand on hers. 'You don't have to tell us if you don't want to.'

For a moment, Jade considered taking Rick at his word. It would be much easier, much less painful, to let Rick and Fi remain in ignorance. But then they would always wonder. 'I don't want to,' she said, 'but you deserve an explanation. Both of you.' She took another sip from the mug.

'When she came to the shop, spying, Linzi Lawson said she knew stuff about me. I don't know how she found out, or what exactly, but she intended to use it against me. If I tell you, I don't have to worry about someone else doing it first.'

'OK,' said Fi, who looked worried.

Jade took a deep breath. 'Daz – Darren – was never mean to me. He never threatened me or hurt me. He was a feckless kid, even though we were both in our twenties. He was fun, a good laugh, but he couldn't settle to a job. He was always dreaming of making it with some scam or scheme. Maybe I went out with him because I dreamed of something better too.' She sighed.

'I lived at home with my mum, just the two of us. My sister Dora got married and moved away, and my dad left when I was ten and didn't visit. Seeing Daz was a break from being at home with Mum, who moaned and fretted and didn't like me going out.' She sipped her tea. 'Then I got pregnant.'

'Hugo,' said Fi.

'Yes. That changed everything.' She paused, remembering how she had felt when the little blue line appeared. 'I thought Daz would dump me when I told him I was pregnant and I was keeping the baby. I thought he'd run away from the responsibility. Turned out he was more enthusiastic than I was. He promised he'd look after us. He got emotional – he cried. Then he got down on one knee and proposed. "Marry me," he said. I told him I'd think about it, but I knew I couldn't marry him.'

'Then Mum found out. Daz's mum rang her – I hadn't told her about the proposal. She'd never liked Daz, didn't think he was good enough for me, but suddenly me marrying him was the best thing since sliced bread. "He can move in with us," she said. "I can help you take care of the baby. Maybe you could even go back to the factory in a year or two, or when baby goes to school."' She shivered, and Rick squeezed her hand.

'I didn't want to go back to the factory. It was boring, packing crisps in boxes. All it had going for it was that the pay was OK and I could walk there in fifteen minutes. I had to take a shower when I got home because I stank of whatever flavour crisps I'd been packing. I'd always dreamed of having my own business one day, being my own boss, but if I married Daz and stayed at home, it would never happen. I'd be stuck for the rest of my life. We'd scrape by and I'd probably end up supporting the family while Daz did dodgy deals or worked cash in hand.'

'So you ran away?' said Fi.

Jade nodded. 'I stuck it out till the end of the month, when I got paid. I closed my bank account, took the cash and packed a couple of cases when Mum was out. Then I went to the train station and bought a ticket to Manchester. I'd never been, so no one would look for me there, and I figured it would be cheaper up north. I left a note saying I was all right and not to worry about me, but I was leaving. When I got to Manchester, I bought a pay-as-you-go mobile and rang Mum every so often to make sure she was OK. I didn't abandon her. She – she—'

'Take your time, Jade,' Rick said softly. 'You don't have to tell us everything now.'

'It turned out she wasn't OK. Not right away. About a year later, she said she'd been getting pains. When I asked how long for, she said months. She hadn't gone to the doctor. When she did, there wasn't much they could do. They gave her a few months, but she collapsed a few weeks later and never came round. I visited her in hospital as often as I could, but I was on the train to Manchester when the hospital rang me.' She drank more tea and swallowed, hard. 'She left me some money which I used to start a business at home. I'd done all sorts – Avon brochures, cleaning catalogues, you name it, I had a round for it. Anything so I didn't have to go home with my tail between my legs.'

'And they never tried to find you?' asked Rick.

Jade shrugged. 'Daz said he didn't, and Mum wouldn't have known where to begin. Anyway, one of the first things I did when I got to Manchester was change my name by deed poll. It's Jane, really. Jane Finch. Could have been worse, I suppose: my sister Dora was christened Dorothy. But I hated it. At school, I was either Plain Jane or Tarzan and Jane. Kids yodelling at me in the playground. I hated school, too. Left as soon as I could.'

'So that's it?' said Fi. 'That's the big mystery?'

'Apart from the failed businesses, the county court judgements when I got behind with the bills, so many fresh starts that Hugo went to a new school almost every year...' She sighed. 'I thought I was doing the right thing. Giving us a better life than if I'd married Daz and stayed at home or gone back to the factory.

But I made the wrong choice, didn't I? I let Hugo down. Daz made something of himself. I just made a mess.'

She wiped away a tear. 'If I'd stayed, Hugo would have had stability and opportunities. Not the chaos he had with me. Now he's met his father and of course, they get on. Hugo says he's not angry, but for all I know, he'll grow to hate me. I can't bear the thought of losing him. The shop I can handle, but Hugo…'

She looked up. Fi and Rick were both watching her, but she couldn't read their expressions. 'You two probably don't want to speak to me any more either. I should go away and be on my own. It's probably safer that way.'

CHAPTER 22

'Oh, Jade,' said Fi. 'Don't even think about leaving. I can't believe you've been carrying that misery all these years.' She reached across the table and took Jade's hand. 'Thank you for finally trusting us. I just wish you'd done it months ago. I was afraid Darren was the murderer and he was threatening you.'

'I'm a terrible person,' sniffed Jade. 'You said I'm a good mother, but I'm not, am I? I dragged Hugo from pillar to post. I didn't let him know his dad or his grandparents. I got in debt. I—'

'Seriously,' said Rick, 'is that the worst secret past you could come up with? Some time I'll tell you about the band's trip along Route 66. Whoo-whee. I can't tell you now or it'd curl Fi's hair.'

'And I can't tell you about my disastrous dates or about slapping my line manager for pinching my backside without making Rick go up in flames,' said

Fi.

Jade gave a brief, wobbly smile then covered her face with her hands. 'It's not the same as getting into debt and – and depriving your child of his family.' Her muffled voice still trembled. 'You didn't have a husband, but you had two sets of parents to help bring up Dylan and give you money if things went wrong financially. When I think of those official envelopes, lying in wait ready to attack, and the rubbish cheap food I fed Hugo, and—'

'Hugo had you,' said Fi, 'and he's turned into a fine young man with fewer hang-ups than most people I know. If you had to buy budget food, so what? Most parents do at some point. It didn't hurt him: now he's a gourmet. Maybe all the moving about made him independent and capable of being his own person without worrying over what anyone else thought. Maybe watching you fight is why he's successful. You were an inspiration. As for debt, you're not alone there.' She stared at the river, then shook herself and texted Hugo and Netta. *We're with Jade. Heading back to Hazeby soon.*

'Fi's right,' said Rick. 'My business won't make me a millionaire any time soon. It's often touch and go as to whether I can carry on. I lived in my van for a while a couple of years ago.'

Jade uncovered her eyes enough to stare at him. 'Really?'

'Yup.'

'But Fi didn't.'

'You know Gavin left me in a lot of debt,' said Fi. 'I nearly lost our house. I had my fair share of official envelopes lying in wait. I could barely afford petrol to go to work and earn money to pay the bills. I know how hard it is to crawl from the red into the black, Jade. I managed to keep ahead of the county court judgments, but only just. Honestly. Yes, my parents could have helped, but that would have stopped them following their own dream, so I didn't tell them. And I couldn't ask Annie and Nigel, because I'd have had to tell them what their son had done. Their hearts were already broken.'

'Everyone comes to a fork in the road at some point and has to decide which way to go,' said Rick. 'Everyone wonders afterwards whether they took the right path. Whatever you do, you still wonder. You were in a difficult situation. You did what felt like the right thing. If you hadn't, you'd never have met me and Fi. That's worth any amount of envelopes.'

'I bet you two never wonder whether you should have taken a different path.'

'I do,' said Fi. 'I wonder what would have happened if I'd put up with Gavin being unfaithful and let him stay. Maybe we'd be divorced, but he'd probably still be alive. I wonder if I've deprived Dylan of a father and siblings. And I wonder what would have happened if I'd stayed in my corporate job instead of starting the Book Barge. I'd probably be senior management. I could have met a rich man, paid for Dylan to go to the best independent school, had a fancy house, designer clothes, the best food…'

'You don't want any of those things.'

'Sometimes I do.' Fi sighed. 'Not the rich man, but sometimes, in the middle of the night, when the Book Barge's expenses are bigger than its income. Or when I open my wardrobe and realise people think I *like* to look plain all the time. Or now that Dylan's older, when I know he'd be more likely to succeed with better connections, and I can't support him through an internship…' Fi cleared her throat and was silent.

'Me too,' said Rick. 'Maybe I could have been a well-paid designer for one of the big companies doing interiors. But mostly…'

'Mostly what?'

'I should have followed you when you stormed off the evening Linzi died. I should have persuaded you to talk to me, and better still, eat dinner. It was a good dinner and you missed it.'

'Come on,' said Fi. 'Let's go to Crystal Dreams. We'll talk things through with Netta, then get petrol for Bertha. I'll be your chauffeur and you can pretend you're royalty in the back.'

They returned to Hazeby without talking, the radio chuntering on low volume. In the rear-view mirror, Fi saw Jade and Rick sitting close and holding hands. Jade had stopped crying.

If only you'd told us, she thought. *If only you'd trusted us. You think I have the perfect family. I don't – no family's perfect. But now I understand why you think that. If I'd been in your position in my early twenties, what would I have done?* The thought sobered her.

What a shame Jade didn't feel anyone would accept her for doing what countless other people have done. Fi had never pried about Hugo's father or Jade's family. The questions she'd asked, to give Jade the chance to explain, had been headed off, and she hadn't wanted to prod. Perhaps she should have, though it might have pushed Jade further away. But maybe now everything was out in the open, Jade could start again properly at last.

Netta threw her arms around Jade as soon as she walked through the door of Crystal Dreams, nearly knocking them both off balance. 'I'm so sorry. I didn't mean what I said. It came out all wrong.'

'Me too,' said Jade, struggling free. 'Except for camomile tea. I still think it's disgusting.'

Netta punched Jade's shoulder gently. 'You don't know what you're missing. Jade, I promise I didn't have anything to do with the murder and I wasn't trying to frame you or anything. You're my friend and my . . . muse. Do I mean muse? Anyway, you've given me the confidence to see what I'm capable of. Maybe I get over-excited, but I want to help you make this business ten times better than Magical Moments, and—'

'OK, OK!' Jade put her hands up in surrender. 'Apology accepted. I'm sorry I took my paranoia out on you. The thing is, that man—'

'Hugo told me. You should have said, Jade. If I'd known who he was, I'd never have said what I did to Rick.' Netta winced. 'Sorry, Rick.'

'Meh,' said Rick. 'No harm done.'

'But... I've been thinking,' said Netta. 'I remembered something which might be important.'

'About Darren?' said Jade.

'No. About the gate. I—'

Despite the closed sign, the shop door burst open and Stan, towing Dylan, rushed to Fi. 'What's going on?' Dylan demanded.

'I thought you were rehearsing.'

'I went home to fetch something and the shop was shut and Stan was on his own. Then someone on the towpath said Crystal Dreams had been shut all afternoon and someone had seen Jade's empty car sat on a verge out of town. I thought— I thought the mur—' He cleared his throat. 'I thought you were here helping her and maybe I could, um, support you.'

'Yes,' said Fi. 'That's what I'm doing and thank you.' But they shared a smile and he briefly touched her shoulder.

'You OK, Jade?' he said, and gave her a lopsided grin. 'More importantly, is Bertha?' All Fi's frustration with him was subsumed by pride in his compassion. 'Still one step ahead of that murderer?'

'I'm OK,' said Jade. 'But I'm not sure we're a step ahead.'

Netta tapped her fingers on the counter and everyone looked her way. 'We might be. On the day the murder happened, I was getting stock from the shed when I heard someone call me from the alley.'

'From the alley?' said Rick.

'That's what I thought. Weird. So I unbolted the gate and peeped out, but I couldn't see anyone. Then Jade called me to hurry up with the stock. I must have forgotten to bolt the gate.'

'Then it's my fault it was unbolted,' said Jade, slumping.

'Of course it's not,' said Netta, firmly. 'It's mine. More importantly, it's just one of those things. Normally, it wouldn't matter.'

Fi's phone vibrated. A video call, from Hugo. She opened it up.

'Is she—' Hugo made an effort to recover his normal elegant nonchalance. 'I mean, is Mummy with you?'

Jade leaned into the frame. 'I'm here. I sort of skedaddled. I don't know how they found me, but they did.'

'Oh, er… Well, I'm super glad you're all right, Mummy. And just to say – and I don't mind saying this in front of people – if it's the tiniest help, I couldn't have had a better mum. Whatever happened, you always put me first. Darren told me a bit about what things were like in your life when you found out I was on the way. If I'd been you, I'd have skedaddled too. I'm glad you did. But please, Mummy, no more skedaddling. Promise?'

'I'll try.'

'Love you.'

'Love you too.'

'Speak later?'

'It might be late.'

'It's never too late.' Hugo blew a kiss and closed the call.

'That's lovely,' sighed Netta. 'But going back to what I said before, an unbolted gate doesn't give anyone an excuse to dump a body in our bin.'

'Our bin?' said Jade. 'I thought you'd be off to start your own business any minute.'

'Nah,' said Netta. 'I love Crystal Dreams. And like I said, you're my friend and my muse.'

'Bleurgh,' said Dylan.

Netta giggled, then looked at her watch. 'There's still a bit of the afternoon left. Shall we reopen?'

'Let's call it a day.' Jade's smile was a little less

wobbly now. 'I've got a car to collect, then we've got a gig to go to while the police do their actual job, so we can stop worrying about the murder and the past and—'

'I'll drink to that,' said Rick.

'Thanks for coming for me. Thank you for – for caring.'

Rick pulled her into a bear hug. 'You're kind of my muse too. I can't have you disappearing.'

'Good grief,' said Dylan. 'You're all worse than Mum and Marcus. I'm off.'

CHAPTER 23

Jade climbed slowly out of sleep. Her head felt muzzy and her ears were still ringing. *It must have been a heck of a night.*

The pillow was firmer than usual, and there was a scent of... She sniffed. Fresh air at the seaside?

'Morning, sleepyhead,' said Rick's voice.

Jade's eyes snapped open. *Of course.*

Rick had walked her home after the gig. 'Thanks,' she had said. 'For everything.'

'I'm just glad you're all right,' Rick replied. 'Now, I have an offer for you.'

Jade smiled. 'Is it an offer I can't refuse?'

'You can if you like: it's entirely up to you. You've had a tough day, and I'm worried you'll get the collywobbles in that flat on your own. So if you want to stay at mine... No, this isn't a trick to get you into bed. You can fetch your hair curlers and a flannel nightie, whatever you like. But if you wake up in the night feeling scared or worried, I don't want you to be alone.'

'My hair curls naturally, thank you very much,' said Jade.

'I suppose the purple bits are natural too.'

'Obviously.' He stood there, smiling at her. 'I'll go and pack a bag.'

Rick's bedroom was plainly furnished but nice: it was certainly tidier than hers. For a moment, Jade wondered if he had planned it. Then she rebuked herself. *You've had enough mean or silly thoughts already today*, she told herself. *Think the best of someone for once, why don't you.*

And here she was, in bed with Rick. At least they were both dressed: she in pyjamas, Rick in a Ramones T-shirt and what she assumed were jogging bottoms.

'Morning,' she said. Her throat was sore, probably from singing along the night before. 'Did you sleep well?'

'I did. You were out like a light ten minutes after your head hit the pillow. I asked you what your favourite song from the gig was. You were thinking about it, then you fell asleep.'

'I hope I didn't snore.'

'I was too busy being asleep to notice.' Jade suspected that meant she had snored and he was too nice to admit it. 'Tea?'

'Yes please.'

'On the way.' He pulled her gently to him and kissed her forehead. Then the bed creaked and she felt the mattress shift as he got up.

Jade rolled on her back and stared at the ceiling. What a day yesterday had been. Yet it had turned out better than she could have imagined. She lay there, smiling gently, until she remembered a murderer was still on the loose. *It doesn't make sense*, she thought. *Linzi Lawson had just arrived in Hazeby. She hadn't had a chance to make enemies. Apart from me, that is, and that was mostly because of her position.*

But we have a lead. The person who called to Netta when she was in the yard can't be a coincidence.

It wasn't much of a lead, though. She'd asked Netta about the voice, but all she could say was that it sounded false. 'It was high and squeaky,' she said. 'When I opened the gate and there was no one there, I assumed it was kids being silly.' Then she shivered. 'But the person knew my name.' She gasped. 'What if it was the murderer?'

'The important thing is that you're safe,' said Jade. 'And no one's after you. They just used you to open the gate. It was a stroke of luck for them that I called you when I did.'

'If I'd remembered to bolt the gate, it might never have happened!' Netta stared up at Jade, her eyes huge.

'You mustn't think that, Netta,' said Jade. 'Linzi Lawson would still have been murdered, but her body would have been dumped somewhere else.'

'I suppose,' said Netta, who nevertheless looked relieved. 'It's still grim, though.'

'It is,' said Jade. 'And I'm going to get to the bottom of it.'

Which, so far, she was failing to do.

'You may want to sit up,' called Rick, and came in with two mugs. 'Here you go.'

'Thanks.' Jade wiggled into a sitting position and sipped her tea. 'I've got murder on my mind.'

'Steady on,' said Rick. 'Some of last night's bands were ropey, but that's a bit harsh.'

'Very funny. I feel as if I can think straight for the first time in weeks. And I want to get whoever did it behind bars where they belong.'

'I appreciate that,' said Rick, getting into bed beside her and thumping his pillow into submission. 'But it's Sunday morning. My brain doesn't get going till the second cup of tea.'

'OK, let me ask you a question. The person who tricked Netta into opening the gate put on a high squeaky voice. What would you think about that person?'

Rick thought. 'I'd assume it was a man, making their voice as different as they could to disguise it.'

'And you say your brain isn't working yet.' She beamed at him and drank more tea. 'The obvious male suspect is Linzi Lawson's husband, Joe. They were separated, but according to the gossip at Magical Moments, she left him.' She frowned. 'So it makes no sense that he would come after her and kill her if he wanted to get back with her.'

'Crime of passion, maybe?' Rick suggested.

'It's possible.' Jade sipped her tea, still frowning. 'But aren't those committed in the heat of the moment? A lot of thought and planning went into Linzi's murder. It doesn't feel right.' She sighed. 'I wish we could find out what the police know.'

She heard a buzz from the bedside table. For a moment, she considered ignoring it. But what if Netta had remembered something else? 'Sorry, I'd better look,' she said, and reached for her phone.

It was a message from Fi. *Are you puzzling over the murder? Because I am.*

Yup, Jade texted back. 'It's Fi,' she told Rick. 'She's thinking about the murder too.'

'Always good to share interests with your friends,' said Rick.

Her phone buzzed again. *Dylan's sleeping at a friend's. Fancy coming for brunch?*

Twenty seconds later, another text. *Marcus is here, by the way.*

Jade's fingers got busy. *Will he help us?*

Hope so. Shall we say ten thirtyish?

Sounds good. Jade paused, her thumb hovering over the *Send* button. 'Rick, Fi's invited me for brunch. We'll probably be talking murder. Would you like to come?'

'Sure, why not?'

Jade resumed her text. *Could I bring Rick?* She pressed *Send*.

Course you can. I assumed he was coming anyway ;-)

***

When Jade and Rick left, they stepped into the sort of crisp, chilly morning that people associate with autumn but rarely happens. More leaves had fallen, and crackled underfoot.

'This feels like a day for solving a mystery,' said Jade.

'Maybe,' Rick replied. 'Or a day for a country walk, maybe a stop at a pub…' He caught her look. 'But let's start with the mystery.'

The lights of the Book Barge were on. They crossed the gangplank and knocked on the wheelhouse door.

'It's open,' called Fi. 'Come on in. I'm making shakshuka.'

Inside, *Coralie* was in Sunday mode and a delicious smell wafted from the galley.

Marcus came into the living area, dressed in jeans

and a maroon sweater and holding a mug of coffee. 'Morning, you two.'

'Morning.' Jade felt rather worried, since she knew Marcus disapproved of her and Fi's sleuthing activities. 'How's your case going?'

'Waiting for information,' said Marcus. 'And as I have a rare day off, I don't plan to say any more. First things first. Tea or coffee?'

They squeezed themselves around the galley table and set about the shakshuka, mopping up tomato juices and egg yolk with warm, crusty bread. Marcus pushed his empty plate away with a happy sigh. 'That was delicious.'

'It was,' said Jade. She wondered what would happen next.

Marcus caught her eye and smiled. 'Normally, I'd be telling you two to stay out of the case. However, Nina has admitted to me that despite following procedure to the letter, she's getting nowhere fast. A knife which could have done the deed was found shoved under the back gate of a shop a few doors down from Crystal Dreams. However, it's clean and of a common make, so no clues there.'

Jade raised her eyebrows. 'So…'

'So, this is in no way official, but if you know anything which might shed light on the Linzi Lawson case and feel disposed to assist the police with their enquiries…'

Jade stood up. 'I'll make more tea.'

Fi cleared the plates and Marcus poured himself and Rick more coffee. A few minutes later, they were settled with their drinks and Marcus had his notebook out. 'Where do you want to begin?'

'I don't think it was the husband,' said Jade.

'No,' said Marcus. 'His alibi for that evening is watertight.'

Jade smiled at this confirmation of her thoughts. 'But we're fairly sure a man's involved. The voice that called Netta in the yard was disguised: a falsetto voice.'

'OK,' said Marcus, making a note. 'And it would be difficult for a woman to get Linzi Lawson into that bin, unless she was both tall and strong.'

'Who might have had a reason to kill Linzi Lawson?' asked Rick.

'The online tributes to her were pretty corporate,' said Fi. 'There was no outpouring of sympathy from her ex-colleagues. Then again, she'd moved on. It doesn't make sense that people she didn't work with any more would make a special trip to Hazeby to murder her.'

'And according to everyone Nina's spoken to, she lived for her work,' said Marcus. 'She had acquaintances – people she chatted to at spin class or Zumba – but no close friends. Her neighbours barely knew her. She spent most of her time with her work colleagues, and when she moved here, she lived in the flat over the shop.'

What a life, thought Jade. 'So if we don't think it's an ex-colleague, it must be someone who works at Magical Moments in Hazeby! But who, and why? They said she made them work hard, but that's no reason to kill someone.'

'You're right,' said Fi. 'There must be something bigger.'

'What about those poisoned chocolates?' said Rick. 'Could someone be on the warpath against the shop itself?'

'That's a point,' said Fi. 'Do we know what was in those chocolates? I assume no one was seriously ill, or the newspapers would have picked it up.'

'Not so far,' said Marcus. 'I'm not sure the analysis report has come back yet.' He fetched his mobile from the worktop. 'I'll send Nina a message. Anyone else, I'd wait till Monday, but Nina…' They watched him type, then heard a whoosh.

'I wondered if the poisoned chocolates were an attempt to put the blame on me,' said Jade. 'I'm the obvious person who benefits if Magical Moments is shut. Given that Linzi Lawson was found with a scarf from my shop…' She looked at Marcus. 'I should probably stop talking, in case it gives you ideas.'

'Who would want to set you up?' Marcus replied.

'That's the thing. While I have occasional paranoid

moments, I can't think of anyone who's actually out to get me. The only person who's threatened me lately is Linzi Lawson herself.' Jade remembered how she had felt when Linzi Lawson said *I know a few things about you, Jade Fitch.* Even now, it made her shiver. But a memory was nagging at her brain. 'Wait a minute. The scarf and the herbs.'

'From your shop, yes,' said Marcus. 'Or not necessarily *from* your shop, but identical to items sold *in* your shop.'

'That's not it. She was stabbed, wasn't she?'

'Yes. The post-mortem found traces of Rohypnol in Linzi's system. It seems likely that her drink was spiked, then she was taken for a walk down the alley to the back of your shop. She was stabbed, the scarf and herbs added for good measure, then put in your bin. As I believe Nina told you, the murderer was lucky and Linzi died almost immediately. Otherwise, she'd have bled to death in the bin. Or maybe she'd have been alert enough to try and get out.'

'That's awful,' said Rick. 'Poor thing.'

'So the scarf and herbs were window dressing,' said Jade. *Didn't Nina say something like that?* 'The murderer could have tied the scarf round her neck, but they didn't. They put it over her mouth as if they were silencing her.'

'What are you saying?' asked Fi.

'When she threatened me, Linzi Lawson seemed

really pleased with herself,' said Jade. 'She'd found some dirt on me, or thought she had, and she intended to use it if she didn't get what she wanted. I reckon she did the same to whoever murdered her.'

'Well now, that's a lead,' said Marcus. His phone buzzed and he checked it. 'Speaking of leads… Nina says the chocolates weren't poisoned as such. They were doctored, but with something very old-school. Ever heard of ipecac?'

Fi frowned. 'That sounds exotic.'

'It's a powerful emetic: makes you sick. It isn't used any more, though: God knows how someone managed to get hold of it. The point is, those chocolates were tampered with to create an effect. Presumably, to divert suspicion from the staff. After all, no one would poison themselves, would they?'

'One person didn't eat any,' said Fi, 'but she's vegan.'

'In that case,' said Jade, 'it probably wasn't her. Too obvious.'

'The other sales assistants were getting stuck into them,' said Fi. 'I don't know about the acting manager…' She frowned. 'He said he'd had one, but I didn't see him eat any.'

'What do you remember of him?' asked Marcus.

'Tall and broad, dark hair, seemed nervous.'

'What was his voice like?' asked Jade.

Fi thought for a moment. 'Quite deep. I wonder…'

'So do I,' said Jade. 'Because with Linzi Lawson gone, he was next in line.' She looked at Marcus. 'I think you should ring Nina. Tell her she's got some digging to do.'

CHAPTER 24

Sheena checked her watch. 'I'm looking forward to this.' She was wearing jeans, a white shirt and a chunky cardigan which showed off her tall, slim figure, with her hair in a long plait. A white scarf patterned with red skulls lay in an elegant twist round her neck. 'It certainly beats Zumba.'

With Netta's help, they'd tracked Sheena down on Sunday afternoon and invited her and her two friends to discuss a plan of action. The three witches had burst into delighted laughter when Jade confessed what she called them.

'You're not wrong,' Sheena said. 'I'm the most experienced, but Vanessa can write a cracking spell and Kim can make a potion, lotion or tea out of anything handy. Thanks to Crystal Dreams.'

'Do they work?' said Fi, intrigued.

'Don't underestimate the power of words,'

answered Vanessa, waving her hand at the bookshelves.

'Or tea,' added Kim, raising her mug. 'But if direct action is required, we can do that too.'

Now, a day later, they had reconvened in the Vine. Fi and Jade sipped soft drinks, while the three witches shared a jug of what was probably sangria, though an irrational part of Fi hoped it was a magic potion.

Vanessa, middle-height and perhaps slightly younger than Sheena, was wearing a burgundy turtleneck sweater over a knee-length floral dress. Her hair was in a neat blonde bob, and she contemplated Fi through her glasses as if reading Fi's mind.

Kim was shorter, perhaps older, definitely plumper. Her outfit was coordinated, but the misty autumn air had frizzed her hair into a curly tangle. 'Right,' she murmured, 'how long do we wait?'

'Ten minutes,' whispered Jade.

'And we've got backup?' whispered Vanessa.

Fi nodded.

'Good,' said Sheena. 'No one messes with Crystal Dreams on our watch.' She gave Jade a reassuring wink.

Fi and Jade slipped out. Despite what she'd said about wanting to wear prettier clothes, Fi felt self-conscious in a floaty navy dress under a navy box jacket. Jade appeared equally uneasy in a grey trouser suit, her hair hidden by a black fedora.

Marcus grinned at them. 'You two look as comfortable as worms in a bird sanctuary. Your outfit's a frill short of wedding attire, Fi, and Jade ought to be wearing spats and carrying a violin case.'

'We have to wear different clothes to normal,' said Fi. 'You've never set foot in Magical Moments, so the staff won't recognise you.'

Jade seemed oblivious to Marcus's teasing. 'I'll go first,' she said, and strode away.

'I was worried you'd be caught up in your other case,' said Fi.

'My team's part is done for now,' said Marcus. 'It's down to the Crown Prosecution Service to decide the charges against the influencer, and whether to link my case with the Met's. So I'm all yours.' He checked his watch. 'Right, I'm off. See you soon.'

Magical Moments was busy when Fi entered a minute later. Harvey was chatting to a man who stood a little beyond the counter, under a sign which said *Remedies*. The customer seemed doubtful. Marcus was peering into the jewellery cabinet. A woman wearing a long raincoat with the hood up contemplated plastic dragons, her back to the counter. Jade's fedora was visible beneath the ceiling sign that said *Talismans*. Hannah and Sonia gossiped at the counter without the remotest interest in anyone.

Fi walked to the crystals, picked up a geode, then

tried on a bracelet. A metre away, Charlie tidied shelves, oblivious to the fact that she could have pocketed valuable merchandise.

The three witches entered in single file, then regrouped. As Fi turned to watch, under the guise of considering the bracelet in a better light, Sheena knocked on the counter. 'Excuse me, is anyone serving?'

'Er, yes,' said Sonia. 'How can I help?'

'Burdock,' said Kim.

'Bless you.'

'It's a root,' said Kim. 'Dandelion would do, at a push. And I need ashwagandha and astragalus. I'm decocting.'

'Does that hurt?' asked Sonia, wide-eyed.

'Decoctions, concoctions and tisanes are all basically herbal tea,' Hannah told her, despite the three witches' bristling. She smiled at Kim. 'We don't stock that sort of stuff here, love. If you go for a walk in the lanes, I bet you can forage it for free.' She swigged her coffee.

'All right, then,' said Sheena. 'Do you have bay, oregano, cinnamon and thyme?'

Sonia puffed out her cheeks. 'We definitely have bay and oregano. Cinnamon, a bit. Thyme, I think we've run out of. Hey, Harv!'

Harvey walked over, frowning, his hands clasped behind his back. 'We'll have a little discussion about protocol later, Sonia. In the meantime, how may I help?'

'She wants thyme. The herb, that is.'

'Lots,' said Sheena. 'Enough to stuff, say, a teapot.'

'We don't stock thyme.' Fi wished she could see Harvey's face properly.

'We usually do,' said Hannah. 'I thought we had loads.'

'There's a little shop in the high street called Crystal Dreams,' said Harvey, ignoring her. 'The woman who runs it will have some. It probably won't be fresh, though: her stock's not great. And in case you don't know…' He leaned forward as if to whisper but kept his voice at the same volume. 'A murder happened there.'

Vanessa shrugged. 'You had poisoned chocolates. I read about it online.'

'Pfft,' said Harvey, 'that was nothing.' Behind his back, his fingers twisted and gripped each other.

'Nothing?' exclaimed Hannah. Her voice roused Charlie, who wandered over, followed by Fi. 'I was as sick as a dog. Those chocolates were laced with . . . what was it, Sonia?'

'Hippy chick?'

'Ipecac,' said Charlie. 'Dreadful, it was.' He shuddered.

'Must have been a fault at the chocolate factory,' said Harvey, unclasping his hands to wave the conversation away. 'Unless that woman at Crystal Dreams did it. Sneaked them in here to poison us. The police should have arrested her. I mean, the body was in her bin.'

'Isn't that slander?' said Vanessa. The three witches moved closer, their eyes boring into Harvey.

He stabbed a finger at Sheena. 'You're one of her customers, aren't you? I recognise that scarf. Linzi told me about the weird stock in that shop. I'm surprised you're still wearing it.'

'Why?' said Sheena, patting the twisted fabric. Fi could tell she was enjoying herself. Jade had sidled up, shielded by a card rack.

'Because that was the scarf—' Harvey put his hands behind his back again.

'Ohhh, because a scarf like that gagged the murder victim?' said Marcus.

'That's it,' said Harvey, looking relieved. 'You must have read that online too, sir.'

'No, the scarf wasn't in any of the news reports. I just guessed what you meant.'

Harvey shrugged. 'In that case, one of the police officers must have told us when we were interviewed.'

'They didn't,' said Hannah. She exchanged puzzled glances with her colleagues.

'They did,' said Harvey.

'No one mentioned a scarf,' said Sonia. Her eyes narrowed with suspicion. 'You're obsessed with

Crystal Dreams, just like Linzi. I remember her sneaking off to do a recce, then vowing she'd run that shop and its owner out of town. And you said you'd help.'

'That wasn't anything to do with Crystal Dreams,' Harvey's neck was blotchy.

'Do tell me more,' said Marcus.

Harvey rounded on him. 'Why do you want to know?'

'Because I'm Detective Inspector Marcus Falconer.' Marcus showed his warrant card, then extracted his notebook. 'Please continue: I'm all ears.'

'We discussed reorganising this shop,' snapped Harvey. 'That's all. My staff can barely remember their names, let alone what happened more than a week ago. They're too busy gossiping about what doesn't concern them.'

Hannah exchanged an angry look with Sonia and thumped her mug down. 'Thanks for nothing.' She turned to Marcus. 'Harvey and Linzi went in the back. I needed shelf labels from the stockroom: I couldn't help overhearing them. Harvey said "What if we planted something?" and Linzi laughed and said "Why not?"'

'We weren't talking about Crystal Dreams at all,' said Harvey. 'The area manager was due the next day and we wanted to surprise him.'

'But you didn't do anything special for the area manager,' said Hannah.

'When was this?' said Marcus.

'Around a week before Linzi got murdered.'

'Ooh, yes,' said Sonia. 'I remember you saying, Han. I didn't think it was to do with the area manager, cos Linzi had just come back from her recce. I thought they were planning to put prawns behind Crystal Dreams's radiators to drive the customers away.'

Everyone stared at her. Then Fi stepped forward, consulting the calendar on her phone.

'Wait a minute,' said Hannah. 'You're—'

'Yes,' said Fi. 'Never mind that now. When was the area manager due? The sixth?'

Harvey ran his finger round his collar. 'Er…'

'Yes,' said Charlie. 'Friday the sixth. I wanted to leave early to take my son to a doctor's appointment and I wasn't allowed, even though Linzi was out for ages the day before, doing that recce.'

'And Linzi died the following Tuesday,' said Marcus.

'Yes,' said Harvey. 'When I was at the pictures.'

'Watching?'

He didn't falter. '*My Big Fat Greek Wedding Three*.'

Marcus flicked through his notebook. 'You booked online and showed Inspector Acaster the e-ticket.'

'Correct.'

'The cinema says the QR code wasn't scanned.'

'Their scanner must be faulty, then,' said Harvey. 'I was there all right.'

'Film any good?' said Marcus. 'What happens?'

'People get married. Obviously. Typical romcom.'

'I don't think you went near the cinema,' said Marcus. 'I think you visited Linzi Lawson in her flat, possibly bringing a bottle of wine, on the pretext of telling her your plan to stitch up Jade. You slipped a drug in her drink to make her compliant, then walked with her to the back of Crystal Dreams. You stabbed her, either in the alley or in the shop's yard, by some fluke killing her instantly. You stuffed herbs in her mouth, gagged her with a scarf like the ones on sale in Crystal Dreams, and dumped her in the bin, in an attempt to throw suspicion on Jade Fitch.'

The customers and staff gasped. Harvey stared round at them. 'There's no evidence.'

'There are a couple of very interesting texts between you and Linzi.'

'You think I'd be stupid enough to text her about…' Harvey ground to a halt. The customers and staff had formed a circle around him, apart from the woman in the raincoat, who was still comparing plastic dragons. 'I've got nothing more to say to you.'

'But I have something to say to you.' The woman in the raincoat put down her hood, revealing herself as

Nina Acaster. 'Harvey Batchelor, I'm arresting you for the murder of Linzi Lawson…'

'But why?' asked Charlie, as Nina recited the caution. 'Just to be manager here? Or did Linzi…' He blushed, then so did Sonia.

Hannah's face was red, too. 'Linzi had something on you too, didn't she?' She turned to Marcus. 'Linzi did that. She found out people's weaknesses and threatened to use them to make their life a misery if they didn't toe the line. Even if it was nothing – like my speeding ticket – she made you feel it was enormous. What was it, Harvey?'

Harvey slumped. 'It wasn't nothing,' he said. 'When I was eighteen, I was convicted for shoplifting and sentenced to community service. My probation officer helped me get on the right path and that conviction was spent years ago. I didn't declare it when I applied for a job with Magical Moments. Somehow, Linzi found out. I was supposed to be the manager in Hazeby while she went to a top job in London. Then she came here instead and took my job. She said it was temporary, while the London job got sorted, but I reckon she'd played her blackmail trick on the wrong person and blown her chances. Anyway, she held that conviction over my head every chance she got. If I didn't toe the line, work overtime, and agree with everything she said, she'd threaten to spill the beans to HQ. Maybe she just got a kick out of making me squirm. But I couldn't stand her having that power over me for the rest of my working life. First I thought of leaving. Then I thought, why should I suffer while she gets away with it yet again?'

Jade took off her hat. 'But why Crystal Dreams?' she said, her face sorrowful. 'Why me? I can see how Linzi got to you, but you don't even know me. Why did you try to pin the murder on me?'

'I should have been the manager here from the start,' Harvey snapped. 'If I had, I'd have finished off your silly little shop in no time. You were just someone to blame.' He turned to Nina and held out his wrists. 'Take me away and get me a solicitor. I'm done.'

'Indeed you are,' said Nina, and clicked on the handcuffs.

CHAPTER 25

Rick frowned at himself in the mirror. 'Should I wear a tie?'

'You're fine as you are,' said Jade. 'Honestly, I thought women were supposed to be the ones who make a fuss.' That said, she had tried on quite a few outfits before settling on a purple velvet dress teamed with the silver moon earrings Hugo had given her last Christmas. She hoped the purple didn't clash too much with her hair.

'It's all right for you,' grumbled Rick. 'You always look nice.'

Jade laughed. 'Even in pyjamas?'

'Especially in pyjamas.' Rick turned back to the mirror. 'Should I do up my top button?'

'Vecchia Pescara isn't that posh,' said Jade. 'The main thing is to make sure your clothes aren't too tight for all the food you'll eat.'

'I didn't think you'd been.'

'Not for a sit-down meal. But I've had their takeaway pizza and that was delicious.' Jade remembered the circumstances under which she and Fi had visited the restaurant and felt her face warm. No need for Rick to know about that…

She came to and realised Rick was watching her, with a strange look on his face. 'Jade, can I say something?'

His expression worried her. She recalled a similar look on Daz's face before he had popped the question. 'We should get moving,' she said. 'Fi and Marcus will be waiting.'

'It won't take a minute. I wanted to say—'

'Can't it wait?' she said, with a mounting sense of desperation.

'I can't say it in public.'

'Rick, maybe now isn't the time to—'

'I'm happy just as we are,' he said. 'I know you did a bunk when Darren proposed to you. In fact, I promise *not* to propose to you, or put any pressure on you to take things faster than you want to.' He huffed out a breath. 'There, I've said it.' Then he looked concerned. 'Was that the right thing to say?'

Jade burst out laughing. 'You had me worried there,' she said, between giggles. 'Come here, you silly man.' She gave him a quick hug. 'Let's get going, before we really are late.'

They wrapped up against the cold and headed down the high street, then into the maze of roads and alleys that was the quickest way to Vecchia Pescara.

Tony Fratelli beamed at them. 'So good to see you, Jade! And your guest! Some of your party are already at the table.'

'Fi and Marcus?' asked Jade.

'That's right. Let me take you through and get you drinks.'

Marcus waved from a circular booth in the corner of the restaurant. Jade was relieved to see that he was wearing a polo shirt, while Fi was in a pretty pale-blue print dress with a navy shrug.

'Now, drinks,' said Tony, rubbing his hands.

'We've got a bottle of red,' said Fi. 'Will you two join us?'

'If that's all right,' said Jade. 'I'll get the next one.'

'I might start with a beer,' said Rick.

Tony recited the list of beers and Rick chose an IPA. 'Very good, sir. One Wyvern's Tail IPA, one extra glass.' He twinkled at them, then turned. 'Livia!' he called.

Jade saw Liv Fratelli sitting at the bar. She slid off her barstool and came over. 'I just wanted to say well done.' She nodded to Marcus. 'It must have been a tricky case, sir.'

'It was, in places,' said Marcus. 'Not that I had much to do with it. You should really be congratulating Inspector Acaster.'

'Of course, sir.' Her grin broadened. 'Credit where credit's due, and all that. I'll let you get on with your evening.'

'No Dylan tonight?' Jade asked Fi.

'Not this time,' said Fi. 'Apparently he's on a coursework deadline.'

'Ah,' said Marcus. 'Leo never mentioned deadlines. Maybe that was the problem.'

'Whatever's brought it on, Dylan's hard at work creating a set design and costumes for a contemporary production of *The Merchant of Venice*. He's pinched my best cardboard box for the stage set, and when I left he was knee deep in fabric samples and wooden dowels.'

'Sounds like he's buckling down,' said Jade.

'For now, yes. And he says he wants to do extra hours in the shop. So I may actually see him outside breakfast time.'

'Good heavens.'

Tony arrived with Rick's beer and a wine glass for Jade. 'Are you ready to order?'

'We'll wait for the others,' said Marcus. 'Could we have some olives and garlic bread in the meantime?'

'Of course!' Tony whisked away.

'I don't suppose you know when Hugo and Netta will put in an appearance?' asked Marcus. 'Assuming they're coming together.'

'They will be,' said Jade. 'They've got things to discuss.'

She thought back to a morning the previous week, when she had got up early and done most of the pre-opening work. Netta had been rather surprised to find the shop unlocked and Jade ready for business when she arrived.

'Netta, can we have a word?' she said, as soon as Netta had closed the door.

Netta looked worried. 'Did I forget something?'

'No, it isn't about that. It's... It's a bit complicated.'

Netta swallowed.

Jade smiled. 'Complicated in a good way. You see, I've come to the conclusion that you're wasted behind the counter at Crystal Dreams.'

Netta gasped. 'But I love it here!'

'I know you do. But one day you'll get bored.'

Netta screwed up her face as if she was bracing for impact.

'So what I'm proposing is to broaden the scope of your role, raise your salary, and give you space to work with other people and do your own projects.'

Netta opened her eyes. 'What?'

'You heard. Your online stuff is doing brilliantly, and with Magical Moments no longer a competitor, our shop sales are going really well too. So there's no reason why I can't invest a bit more in your side of the business. However, at the moment that isn't a full-time role, so what I propose is that you work three days a week for me. Hugo's interested in getting you to do some work for him, and I bet you have ideas of your own that you'd work on if you had the time.'

'But – but who will run the shop?'

'Me. And we can afford – not a Saturday girl, but extra part-time help.'

Sheena had been delighted when Jade invited her into the back room for a quick chat. 'Me?' she said. 'I'd be honoured.'

'I haven't quite decided about hours,' said Jade. 'Those could be flexible. I can certainly give you an idea of duties and salary.'

'One question,' said Sheena. 'Will there be a staff discount?'

Jade thought. 'There certainly could be, and perhaps an incentive scheme. I'll get the kettle on. I've got normal tea, decaf and camomile.'

'Normal tea, please,' Sheena said decisively. 'Can't abide camomile.'

'A woman after my own heart,' said Jade, and put the kettle on.

Yes, Sheena will be a great addition to the team...

Rick nudged her and she returned to the present. 'Here they are at last!' he said.

Netta and Hugo were weaving their way between the tables. Netta was willowy in a black spaghetti-strap dress, while Hugo was resplendent in navy chinos, a pink shirt, a purple cravat patterned with white horses and a sports jacket.

'Sorry we're late,' Hugo announced to the table. 'Netta and I were talking business and forgot the time.' Marcus rolled his eyes. Jade actually believed them.

'Oh yes?' said Fi.

'I've agreed to work one day a week for Hugo,' said Netta. 'And Jade's getting extra help in the shop to cover me working on the online business. Which will *grow*.'

'Gosh,' said Marcus. 'All change, then.' He turned to Jade. 'So you're expanding the evil empire?'

'I am,' said Jade. She'd already discussed it with Rick and Fi, and when they weren't in the middle of a busy restaurant she'd tell Marcus, assuming Fi hadn't already.

It had all begun, as things often seemed to, with a video call from Hugo. 'Mummy, I want to talk to you about money.'

Jade winced. 'I'd rather not, Hugo.'

'That's the problem. You're trapped in a scarcity mindset.'

'You what?'

'Oh, Mummy. You always think you'll run out of money, or that the bank will never lend you any. I don't think that's true.'

'Well, I've got money in the bank, but—'

'I'm sure those CCJs you had must have expired. Unless there's some I don't know about,' he said, with a severe expression.

'No there aren't, you cheeky blighter. What do you mean, they expire?'

'Exactly. Now, my dad's consulting in Wyvernton next week and he said it would be no trouble to pop to Hazeby one evening and go through your finances with you. Not a judgement thing, just to help you out. It will be a good opportunity for you to talk without arguing, too. So I told him seven pm on Tuesday and you'll cook. He doesn't eat red meat, but otherwise, anything.'

The result, after a vegetarian lasagne and two alcohol-free beers as Darren was driving, was that they managed to have a sensible conversation and Jade discovered her credit score was nowhere near as bad as she had thought. 'You've actually done most things right lately,' said Darren. 'You've settled bills on time, you've taken out credit cards and kept up on payments, and overall, things are looking good. You could take out a business development loan if you wanted. You could also consider taking out a mortgage and getting your own place. That would be cheaper than renting, and you'd gain an asset.'

'Really?'

He smiled. 'Yes, really.'

'I... I don't know what to say. Apart from thank you.'

His smile broadened. 'You're very welcome.'

And ever since, she had had pleasant dreams about being a woman of property.

I could say goodbye to that rat Mr Snead, she thought, as she sipped her wine. *I could move to a bigger shop. I could buy a place of my own. Or...* She glanced at Rick, who was laughing at something Marcus had said.

Suddenly her phone buzzed: a video call. She was about to reject it when she saw the name on the display. She stood up. 'Sorry everyone, I need to take this. Can someone order me a lasagne, please, when Tony comes back?'

Fi raised her eyebrows, and Jade nodded. *Good luck*, mouthed Fi.

Jade hurried to the vestibule, composed herself, and pressed *Answer*.

A woman appeared on screen. She was a few years older than Jade, tanned, her dark curly hair streaked with blonde. And she had Jade's features. 'I hope this isn't the middle of the night for you,' she said. 'I can never work out the time difference.'

'Hi, Dora,' said Jade. 'I'm in a restaurant, but it's fine. The food will be a while.'

Dora grinned at her, and it was like looking in the mirror. 'You haven't changed a bit.'

WHAT TO READ NEXT

If you've enjoyed reading Fi and Jade's fifth case together, here's a little about the next book in the series: *Death in a Dinner Jacket*.

Save the last dance for death…

When Marcus is invited to a high-school reunion, he's looking forward to catching up with old friends. Fi is delighted as she'll get the chance to dress up and show her feminine side. Jade is less enthusiastic and there's no way she'll wear a ball dress, even for Rick.

Former classmates convene on Hazeby – those who stayed, and those who left as soon as they could. Friendships are rekindled and the party is a great success until the body of a guest is discovered with the apparent murderer standing nearby. What possible motive could they have?

As Marcus investigates, he realises that rivalries and abandoned love affairs have been rekindled too.

Could these be behind the murder? But he's hampered by his emotions and his son Leo's friendship with the main suspect.

It's down to Fi and Jade to help find the killer before the wrong person is charged and their life is ruined.

Check out *Death in a Dinner Jacket* here: http://mybook.to/DeathDJ.

If you've enjoyed reading a co-written book, *Caster and Fleet Mysteries* is a six-book series we wrote together, set in 1890s London. Meet Katherine and Connie, two young women who become friends in the course of solving a mystery together. Their unlikely partnership takes them to the music hall, masked balls, and beyond. Expect humour, a touch of romance, and above all, shenanigans!

The first book in the series is *The Case of the Black Tulips,* and you can read all about it here: http://mybook.to/Tulips.

If you love modern cozy mysteries set in rural England, *Pippa Parker Mysteries* is another six-book series set in and around the village of Much Gadding.

In the first book, *Murder at the Playgroup*, Pippa is a reluctant newcomer to the village. When she meets the locals, she's even more reluctant. There's just one problem: she's eight months pregnant.

The village is turned upside down when a pillar of the community is found dead at Gadding Goslings playgroup. No one could have murdered her except the people who were there. Everyone's a suspect, including Pippa…

With a baby due any minute, and hampered by her toddler son, can Pippa unmask the murderer?

Find *Murder at the Playgroup* here: http://mybook.to/playgroup.

Finally, if you love books and magic, welcome to the *Magical Bookshop*! This six-book series combines mystery, magic, cats and of course books, and is set in modern London.

When Jemma James takes a job at Burns Books, the second-worst secondhand bookshop in London, she finds her ambition to turn it around thwarted at every step. Raphael, the owner, is more interested in his newspaper than sales. Folio the bookshop cat has it in for Jemma, and the shop itself appears to have a mind of its own. Or is it more than that?

The first in the series, *Every Trick in the Book*, is here: http://mybook.to/bookshop1

ACKNOWLEDGEMENTS

As always, our first thanks go to our marvellous beta readers – Carol Bissett, Ruth Cunliffe, Christine Downes, Stephen Lenhardt and Julia Smith – and to our eagle-eyed proofreader, John Croall. Thank you very much for your help! Of course, any errors that remain are our responsibility.

And many thanks to you, dear reader! We hope you've enjoyed the latest instalment in Fi and Jade's adventures. If you have, please consider leaving a short review or a rating on Amazon and/or Goodreads. Reviews and ratings are very important to authors, as they help books to find new readers.

COVER CREDITS

Image: fallen figure from Depositphotos, triangle (recoloured) from clker.com.

Cover fonts:

Fairing by Design and Co.

Dancing Script OT by Impallari Type: https://www.fontsquirrel.com/fonts/dancing-script-ot. License: SIL Open Font License v1.10: http://scripts.sil.org/OFL.

ABOUT LIZ HEDGECOCK

Liz Hedgecock grew up in London, England, did an English degree, and then took forever to start writing. After several years working in the National Health Service, some short stories crept into the world. A few even won prizes. Then the stories started to grow longer...

Now Liz travels between the nineteenth and twenty-first centuries, murdering people. To be fair, she does usually clean up after herself.

Liz's reimaginings of Sherlock Holmes, her Pippa Parker cozy mystery series, the Caster & Fleet Victorian mystery series (with Paula Harmon), the Magical Bookshop series, and the Maisie Frobisher Mysteries are available in ebook and paperback.

Liz lives in Cheshire with her husband and two sons, and when she's not writing or child-wrangling you can usually find her reading, messing about on

Twitter, or cooing over stuff in museums and art galleries. That's her story, anyway, and she's sticking to it.

Website/blog: http://lizhedgecock.wordpress.com
Facebook: http://www.facebook.com/lizhedgecockwrites
Twitter: http://twitter.com/lizhedgecock
Goodreads: https://www.goodreads.com/lizhedgecock

ABOUT PAULA HARMON

Paula Harmon is a civil servant, living in Dorset, married with two adult children. Paula has several writing projects underway and wonders where the housework fairies are, because the house is a mess and she can't think why.

For book news, offers and even the occasional recipe, please sign up to my newsletter via my website.

https://paulaharmon.com
viewauthor.at/PHAuthorpage
https://www.facebook.com/pg/paulaharmonwrites
https://www.goodreads.com/paula_harmon
https://twitter.com/Paula_S_Harmon

BOOKS BY LIZ HEDGECOCK

To check out any of my books, please visit my Amazon author page at http://author.to/LizH. If you follow me there, you'll be notified whenever I release a new book.

The Magical Bookshop (6 novels)
An eccentric owner, a hostile cat, and a bookshop with a mind of its own. Can Jemma turn around the second-worst secondhand bookshop in London? And can she learn its secrets?

Pippa Parker Mysteries (6 novels)
Meet Pippa Parker: mum, amateur sleuth, and resident of a quaint English village called Much Gadding. And then the murders began…

Booker & Fitch Mysteries (5 novels, with Paula Harmon)
Jade Fitch hopes for a fresh start when she opens a new-age shop in a picturesque market town. Meanwhile, Fi Booker runs a floating bookshop as well as dealing with her teenage son. And as soon as they meet, it's murder…

Caster & Fleet Mysteries (6 novels, with Paula Harmon)
There's a new detective duo in Victorian London . . . and they're women! Meet Katherine and Connie, two young women who become partners in crime. Solving it, that is!

Mrs Hudson & Sherlock Holmes (3 novels)
Mrs Hudson is Sherlock Holmes's elderly landlady. Or is she? Find out her real story here.

Maisie Frobisher Mysteries (4 novels)
When Maisie Frobisher, a bored young Victorian socialite, goes travelling in search of adventure, she finds more than she could ever have dreamt of. Mystery, intrigue and a touch of romance.

The Spirit of the Law (2 novellas)
Meet a detective duo – a century apart! A modern-day police constable and a hundred-year-old ghost team up to solve the coldest of cases.

Sherlock & Jack (3 novellas)
Jack has been ducking and diving all her life. But when she meets the great detective Sherlock Holmes they form an unlikely partnership. And Jack discovers that she is more important than she ever realised...

Tales of Meadley (2 novelettes)
A romantic comedy mini-series based in the village of Meadley, with a touch of mystery too.

Halloween Sherlock (3 novelettes)
Short dark tales of Sherlock Holmes and Dr Watson, perfect for a grim winter's night.

For children
A Christmas Carrot (with Zoe Harmon)
Perkins the Halloween Cat (with Lucy Shaw)
Rich Girl, Poor Girl (for 9-12 year olds)

BOOKS BY PAULA HARMON

THE MURDER BRITANNICA SERIES
Murder Mysteries set in 2nd Century Britain
mybook.to/MurderBritanniaSeries

THE MARGARET DEMERAY SERIES
Historical Mysteries set in the lead-up to World War 1
mybook.to/MargaretDemeraySeries

OTHER BOOKS BY PAULA HARMON
https://paulaharmon.com/books-by-paula-harmon/

SHORT STORIES BY PAULA HARMON & VAL PORTELLI
viewbook.at/PHWeirdandpeculiartales

AUDIOBOOKS BY PAULA HARMON
https://paulaharmon.com/audiobooks/

WHITE RHINO BOOKS

Printed in Great Britain
by Amazon